Evelyn

THE CUPID CHRONICLES

BY KALLIE ROSS

Have you read *Unbreakable*, the next book in The Cupid Chronicles?

KALLIE ROSS

UNBREAKABLE

THE CUPID CHRONICLES

Learn more at
www.TheCupidChronicles.com

KALLIE ROSS

Evelyn

THE
CUPID
CHRONICLES

Evelyn: A Cupid Chronicles Novella
By Kallie Ross
Copyright © 2016 by Kallie Ross
All Rights Reserved

ISBN 978-0-9983532-1-0 (paperback)

Edited by Maria Pease, The Paisley Editor.

Cover Art by Drew Rodgers at Living Stone Design.

First Edition: 2016

Dedicated to the act of love.
Because actions speak louder than words.

Chapter One

"What the crap?" Evelyn squinted in the direction of the majestic St. Louis Cathedral. Slapping the iron-laced balcony, she couldn't believe the view of the French Quarter. The leaves were turning yellow, and humid air blew in from the lake. "Who in the Heavens had the bright idea to bring me back here? I could've told you this was a bad idea."

"You know the Elders would not have sent us if it were not imperative. They deliberated for several days over the message they received." Andel Lambros, Evelyn's Cupid-mentor, was all warrior-Cupid, all of the time. He had been vague about the mission they were on.

Evelyn's first mission.

Before this, Andel had trained Evelyn for weeks in the Heavens. She'd been unaware an entire year had passed on earth. Finding herself in the heavens, would have been freaky enough. But after shoving the love of her life, Tate Gallier, out of the way of a speeding trolley, she was more ticked off.

When she found out she'd be going back to earth, Evelyn attempted to hone her archery skills. But hitting a target with a stick had been harder than it looked. Especially with Andel constantly instructing her. For being dead she felt better than ever, except her heart. It was decimated.

Evelyn's eyesight went from 20/80 to perfection. Her oily T-zone transformed into a peaches-and-cream complexion. And with every training exercise, she was acutely aware of her growing strength and improving agility. Even with her heavenly upgrade, she felt anger boiling in her core.

She'd become immortal. As a full-fledged Cupid, like Andel, she would have to hold up her end of an eternal covenant. Piercing hearts with true love. Two at a time, couples like she and Tate, for the unforeseeable future.

"Bring the undying arrow which pierced two hearts, yet only remains in one," Evelyn recited the cryptic message an octave lower than her normal voice. The Elders had given Andel and her the riddle. Fulfilling the prophecy would be necessary if she ever wanted to become a full-fledged Cupid. "I can barely hit the practice targets, and I haven't even shot an arrow at a human yet. Do you think I'll miss or accidentally hit the wrong people?"

Andel rolled his green eyes, proof that he'd reached his limit with Evelyn's questions. Who chose her? What did she do to deserve becoming a heavenly being? Would she make a good Cupid? Why was it necessary she have a babysitter, a.k.a. Andel? Was immortality going to be worth it?

Andel didn't question whether Evelyn was ready for her first assignment. He hoped the Elders had deciphered the message correctly, because once he revealed Evelyn target there would be no turning back.

"The arrow in question was shot before you became a Cupid, Evelyn."

"Okay, so why don't *you* just go get it?"

Another question. It sent Andel pacing the balcony of their newly acquired apartment. As much as she complained, she had not said one negative thing about their temporary living arrangement. The two-bedroom Pontalba Apartment had hardwood floors, French Country decor, and a view of Jackson Square. It was the perfect place to live in Evelyn's eyes. She thought she heard Sandra Bullock owned one when she'd lived in the city as a college student.

"Cupids do not create love, we…"

"Assist it," Evelyn finished with her own eye roll. "Blah, blah. Blah-dee, blah, blah."

Andel's hands squeezed into fists on the railing that faced the park's walkways. His arrow tattoo twitched along his forearm. The restraint he practiced had been maturing for the past 200 years. Something about Evelyn's apathy toward a Cupid's calling threatened to crack his reserve. If it weren't for his ability to see Evelyn's heart, he might have given up on her entirely.

"How about we take a walk?" Andel wasn't asking. He placed his hand over Evelyn's, and with the thought of the wrought iron fences and street lamps below, Andel transported them to Jackson Square.

Poof.

No one around them was the wiser and the two Cupids fell in step with the afternoon crowd. As they strolled through the historic tourist attraction, Evelyn felt a whisper of something heavenly. She quickly dismissed it as residual power coming from Andel.

"I can't wait to learn that trick." Evelyn resented appearing wherever Andel allotted her to be.

"It is not learned. In the same way your aim with an arrow will become natural, you will acquire all a Cupid's powers. They come with accepting your new role, and your immortality."

It wasn't enough that Evelyn gave up her life for her boyfriend. She also had to pierce her first hearts to prove herself. If she didn't complete the task she'd end up taking a trip into the white light.

"Has it occurred to any of you that I might not want to live forever? Especially with a know-it-all mentor who's more boring than my Intro to Philosophy class."

"Ouch. I get it. Being a Cupid is still a tough concept to wrap your mind around." Andel stopped in the middle of the path.

Pedestrians sidestepped around them without protesting, because Andel emitted love. The feeling was like a warm and fuzzy cushion surrounding his chiseled form. And as resentful as Evelyn was, she couldn't resist its lulling comfort. After flexing his Cupid power, she was no longer pissed. He made her feel safe, and he was too handsome to stay frustrated with for any length of time.

"It's not that simple. I may prove I'm worthy of becoming a Cupid, but what if I don't want to spend an eternity assisting love? It's the one thing I can't have. I don't think seeing the love of my life after dying is going to turn out the way you hope." Evelyn turned and started walking again. "The Elders expect me to get over what happened and bless some random couple with love. And, in the same city that all my friends are in. What if I'm recognized? What if I see Tate? It's too much."

Andel swallowed down what he knew he'd have to confess. He moved to catch up with Evelyn, and resorted to a diversion to buy himself some time. "No one here will recognize you because you do not look like yourself."

"So we're like angels in disguise, or something?"

"Or something. One of the gifts we have is cloaking our physical presence. While I have dark hair, I can appear to have golden curls to the humans around us. I have the ability to cover you in the same cloak, as well as wrap the both of us with our surroundings."

"And I'll be able to do that too?" Evelyn asked, watching the crowd take in the fountain at the center of the square. The people ignored the two Cupids. It was like they were invisible.

"You will. Of course, you must prove your loyalty to our immortal race by piercing your first two hearts. And, fulfill the prophesy."

"*And*? You mean they're not the same thing? I thought my mission was to pierce two hearts."

"Not entirely. We must focus on acquiring the arrow first. If we do not make the offering, that is, the arrow-- in time, then it will not matter if you pierce your first couple. Our immortality, along with our other powers, will no longer exist. *We* will no longer to exist."

"No pressure." She rolled her eyes.

"Evelyn, you need to understand that time is a peculiar device. Between the heavens and the earth, time dissolves, and…"

"*And* get on with it. Are we Time Lords or something? Do I have two hearts now?"

A sax player loosened his fingers along the keys of his instrument, startling Evelyn. The lilting tune entertained the passersby and distracted Evelyn for a few minutes.

Waiting until the music faded, Andel informed, "It's been a year. You have been gone a year, training in the heavens."

Evelyn walked away, and Andel rushed to catch up. They fell into a silent rhythm with the sounds of the street moving through the square. Evelyn wrestled with the difference in time from one realm to the other. It reminded her of the one-way streets downtown. If you didn't pay attention you'd miss your turn and get stuck going the wrong direction.

Evelyn had lived in New Orleans as a college student at Tulane University and walked this street several times. It didn't look any older. If Andel was telling the truth, and Evelyn didn't think he could lie, it had been three years since she'd moved to the city.

On her first day, at Freshman Orientation she'd sat next to Tate Gallier. After their fifth date, she knew. He'd dropped her off at her dorm, and after revealing more about her past than she'd intended he held her. While she breathed in his soapy scent, he rubbed his hands along her back in a calming motion. It was in that moment she distinguished a change in their relationship. It wasn't merely Tate's transition from friend to boyfriend. Evelyn and Tate were both struck by something deeper.

They dated a year before it all came to an end. The irony wasn't lost on Evelyn. Her life wouldn't have come to an abrupt stop if the trolley had.

Umph.

"Pardon me," a stranger grumbled after knocking shoulders with Evelyn.

"Wha-How?" Evelyn turned full-circle to find Andel leaning against a lamppost smirking.

"I pulled the cloak. You were daydreaming, and I need you here, now. There is more I need to tell you, but it will be best for you to sit down."

He placed a hand on her shoulder, and *poof.*

In a flicker, Andel and Evelyn were sitting at a table in Cafe Pontalba. The Cajun restaurant bustled with hungry guests. It sat below their apartment and Evelyn had spent the morning breathing in garlic, onion, and oregano.

"What can I get the two of you to drink?" A full-figured, blonde tapped her pen on a pad of paper covered in scribble. She wore an apron with a name badge introducing herself as Sabine. She avoided eye contact with Evelyn but didn't mind getting a good long look at Andel.

"*I* will have some water and the biggest piece of chocolate cake you've got," Evelyn answered.

"Sure. And for you, sweetheart?"

"I will have some spicy boiled shrimp to start off and a glass of Riesling. Thank you, Sabine."

"You got it." With a wink and sway of her hips, Sabine made her way to the bar.

Evelyn was glad to know she could walk downstairs for a sugar fix. Their apartment stored everything they needed; bows, arrows, and clothes. Whoever set the place up stocked a cabinet in the living room full of their Cupid gear. Evelyn had glimpsed quivers full of arrows on her way to check out the bedrooms. One of the closets was full of clothes for her. The jeans and tops weren't much different than the ones she wore when she was human. Each piece had a semblance of toughness, but instead of lace or crocheted trim there was leather. Bows replaced with buckles.

"I cannot wait for that cake. There should be chocolate in the Heavens. So, can Cupids drink wine and eat shrimp? I mean, you're at least 26 or 27, even if you act like your 65, but I've never seen you eat, let alone drink alcohol."

"I am 24, and I have explained we do not have to eat. But, we can enjoy Cajun shrimp. When in Rome... But this is not important." Andel waved his hand over the table. "We need to discuss the mission."

"Shoot." Evelyn pulled an imaginary string back from an imaginary bow like she was shooting an arrow.

"This is serious, Evelyn."

Sabine returned with their drinks and set a steaming bowl in front of Andel. Placing a plate of chocolate cake in front of Evelyn, the waitress didn't pause to bat her eyelashes or ask if they needed anything else. It only bothered Evelyn because she felt the urge to order another slice of cake. She had missed chocolate. The reason the waitress had overlooked Andel was the sudden appearance of his mystic glamour. Evelyn felt its caress extending over her. The cloak hadn't made them invisible, but it created the illusion that they were less interesting.

"We're on a time crunch. A year of my afterlife has evaporated, and now I'm going to retrieve an arrow from some sap that's still in love with his old flame." Evelyn spouted.

"Not exactly."

The prophesy had been relatively clear. *Bring the undying arrow which pierced two hearts, yet only remains in one.* Evelyn didn't have a clue who the message referred to, but the Elders were adamant she was the only one who could claim the arrow.

Andel had taken on the charge of training her, the new Cupid, before the message had been delivered. He'd grown impatient with Evelyn each day during target practice. Her heavy grief caused each arrow she shot to fall short of its mark. He knew healing from the loss of Tate would take more time than Evelyn had. In the last few weeks, her heartache had transformed into cynicism, and Andel took the brunt of it.

Evelyn shoved a forkful of cake into her mouth to ensure she didn't ask another question. Andel's eyebrows inched together, and Evelyn had gathered he was either annoyed or being stoic. The less she said the better.

"Usually, a Cupid's arrow will pierce two hearts and they are only separated by death. Our job is not only to affix true love, but to fight for it." Andel's jaw clenched, and he resembled a perfect marble statue. They were warriors, fighting for the purest act that ever existed. If they didn't make the offering, darkness would destroy love forever.

Not able to restrain herself any longer, Evelyn blurted, "If we're fighting for love, then why would we pull the arrow out of a person and offer it to some greater power?"

"There is not an easy way to explain it, but the young man suffering can find love again if we retract the arrow. The Elders believe his undying love is the one referred to in the message. It will not be easy to get close enough to remove it, and you may find the situation distressing. Remember, I am here to help you."

Andel took a sip of his wine, and he looked as if he could be drinking amongst royalty. With a wave of his hand, two twenty dollar bills appeared on the table. Before Evelyn could take another bite of the soul-soothing chocolate, she faced her past.

Poof.

Tate Gallier sat in a crowded university classroom in the front row. Evelyn stood before them all, wishing she still had that cake to hide behind. Andel was at her side dressed in a dark, tailored suit. "Welcome, class. You have arrived in Human Behavior and Social Environment. I'm Dr. Andel Lambros and this is my assistant, Cordelia Hunt. Let's get started."

Evelyn couldn't see the glamour disguising her and Andel, but she could feel it. Being concealed didn't subside the anxiety flooding her. It felt like water slowly filled her lungs as the fear of being discovered overwhelmed her.

If she'd gotten her chocolate fix, Evelyn might not have been so sick to her stomach. But, then again, a full stomach would have been another, more obvious problem. To avoid coming eye to eye with Tate Evelyn glared at Andel. Knowing he sat a few feet away, her heart twisted in her chest.

She would have to remove the arrow from Tate's heart, or at least the half that he held on to. When she died for him she had no idea he would hold on to their love for so long. It was unfair that the Cupid elders expected her to rip away the love they had pierced them with. She didn't think she could do it, especially all by herself.

Chapter Two

"Class dismissed." From his podium, Dr. Andel Lambros straightened a pile of papers that looked more like a game of 52 Card Pickup. After an hour of academic torture, the students made their escape. Evelyn had undergone emotional torment while faced with Tate. He'd worn his hair a little longer than she remembered, but could never forget those old black Converse.

Evelyn wasn't sure how Andel had done it. He'd convincingly introduced the junior-level course she would have taken if she hadn't died. As he taught, Andel had paced along the front of the lecture hall. Evelyn had been stuck sitting at a desk facing thirty-or-so college students and Tate. When she managed to pry her eyes off of him, she watched Andel.

The light would catch the Cupid at a certain angle and Evelyn thought she saw what every student perceived him to be, a professor. It wasn't much different than what she'd grown accustomed to gazing at during training. He'd used glamour to age himself. He didn't look anywhere near his real age, somewhere around 224. But with the salt and pepper curls and accentuated frown lines, he could pass for early fifties.

Once the room was clear Evelyn began, "What the—"

"Language," Andel reminded. The first time they met, he'd gone on and on about how a lady should speak. Persisting even after a stunt like that, she thought she deserved a cuss word.

"Language? Are you kidding me? After all I've had to process in the last few weeks what makes you think *poofing* me in front of Tate was a good idea?"

"None of it is a good idea if you ask me, but it must be done." Andel ran his fingers through his hair and avoided eye contact. "If not just now, then when? And *poofing*? Call it *transcending*."

"I don't care what you call it. I'd prefer it if you'd ask first, or at least use a code word to warn me in the future."

"That can be arranged. I will use the word *adieu*."

"Fine." Evelyn crossed her arms.

"Now, off you go. You need to get close to Tate if we have any chance of pulling this off."

"Get close? That's what got me into this mess to begin with. I don't think I can confront him. I miss him. I love him. And I don't want to rip that love out of him. I died for that love."

"Evelyn, few have ever sacrificed their life for another."

"Exactly." Evelyn gritted her teeth, preparing for the heavenly lecture she knew was coming.

"Exactly," Andel agreed. He twisted his lips in thought. Forced to come face to face with everything she'd been torn away from, he knew she would have to leave it all behind again when this was over.

"What are you playing at, Cupid?" Evelyn raised an eyebrow in question.

"Nothing. Think about it. You gave your life for Tate before. Why wouldn't you do it again?"

Like being doused with icy water, Andel's words shocked Evelyn's senses into awareness. Her shoulders tightened, ready for the next move. "Point taken."

"Very well then, *Adieu.*"

Poof.

Evelyn's eyes widened and she stared back at her reflection, but they weren't her eyes. Andel had *poofed* her to the ladies' room and she was standing in front of a sink and mirror. A stall door swung open behind her, and a girl her age stepped up to the sink next to her. Lathering her cocoa-colored skin she smiled, then reached around Evelyn and struck a conversation.

"Hi."

"Uh, hi." Evelyn reached up and pressed her palms to her cheeks. She couldn't believe the glamour gawking back at her. She ran her fingers through what was usually long, chestnut brown hair. The girl in her reflection had red hair. Shoulder length red hair. Her face appeared heart-shaped, and her normally thin upper lip was plump with a perfect Cupid's bow. Andel's cloak, or whatever it was, resembled the superhero-chick in the Avengers movies.

Placing hands on her hips, the girl next to her winked and asked, "So can you tell me anything about Dr. Lambros? Is this class going to kick my butt?"

Evelyn, startled by her new face, stuttered. "Oh. Uh. Well, I'm not sure. This is the first time I've worked with him." Evelyn recovered after realizing Dr. Lambros was Andel. "I heard that he drones on like that every time he's train... I mean teaching."

Both girls exited into the hallway and came face to face with Tate, Andel, and another guy she recognized but couldn't place.

"Cordelia Hunt. Just who I was looking for," Andel addressed Evelyn and encouraged her to play along with a wink.

She felt torn in two. Evelyn wanted to hold Tate close, but he seemed so far away. "Yes, Sir?"

"This is Tate Gallier and Jeremy Rogers." With the introduction, Jeremy, the lanky stranger, laid eyes on Evelyn's new acquaintance. Jeremy didn't acknowledge anyone else, and Tate only had eyes for his untied shoelace.

"It's nice to meet you. This--" Evelyn nodded, but stalled when she waved to introduce the girl who stood next to her.

"I'm Autumn Bassett." The girl's ring-clad hand reached forward and shook Tate's hand. "It's a pleasure to meet you both and you too, Dr. Lambros."

Autumn let go of Tate's hand, and when she touched Jeremy, Evelyn's heart sang. She knew it was their first meeting, but her soul soared at their epic connection. When they released hands, the sound of the orchestra faded into the serenade of a string quartet. Autumn held her hand out to shake Andel's, but his hands remained in his pockets.

"Yes. Thank you." Andel's refusal came off as a germaphobic snob. "Cordelia, these gentlemen have asked about organizing a study group. Since there is an odd number of students in the class, I would like for you to join them."

"Autumn, you're welcome to join us, too," Jeremy butted in. The tempo of Evelyn's heart's song sped up.

"Thanks, I might just do that." She lifted her chin and grinned.

"I have given Tate your contact information, and he will let you know when they intend to meet." Andel turned and walked away from the college students. After a year, Evelyn felt she was where she belonged. Autumn snickered at the sterile departure, a contagious sound. After the classroom door shut behind him, they all laughed, releasing some tension and apprehension.

"So I'll text you at a specific time," Tate offered. "But Jeremy and I were thinking of getting together tomorrow morning." Evelyn blanched at the idea of having to get up too early. Becoming immortal didn't mean she was willing to give up her down comforter and alone time. "I have a class until 8 tomorrow night." Tate explained as he pulled his cell phone out of his pocket.

"Tomorrow morning works best for me," Autumn interjected. She grabbed her phone out of her messenger bag. "Why don't you give me your number, Jeremy?"

Autumn's flirting brought a smile to Evelyn's face. For a moment, she thought being a Cupid wouldn't be so bad. Having to wake up early would be a pain, but the sooner she could get the arrow, the sooner she could save the Cupids.

After playing superhero, she could take her time choosing the mark, or couple, who would seal her deal with the Elders. Eventually, with some experience, she'd go out on missions without a muscle-bound-poofing-partner.

Buzz-buzz.

Evelyn flinched. Slipping her hand into her back pocket, she pulled out a phone that hadn't been there a minute earlier. She knew she hadn't felt Andel place the phone in her pocket by hand, and if she had he would have lost said hand.

A message filled the screen.

Tate Gallier, human behavior study group, 9am @ PJ's.

Evelyn's gaze swung to Tate and he gave her a crooked grin.

"Come on, Jer. Let's get going." Tate started walking away before Jeremy handed back Autumn's phone.

Even with the half-smile, Tate hadn't shown an interest in Evelyn's alter ego, Cordelia. She knew Tate's moves. Her disguise appeared airbrushed, like she could walk onto a movie set and play Channing Tatum's love interest.

The fact that he didn't flirt with a girl, that wasn't her, should have made her happy. Instead, it felt like a bowling ball dropped into her stomach. If Evelyn dead and buried, Tate should have at least flirted. The void of emotions surrounding him indicated something was seriously off with him.

Autumn nudged Evelyn with her elbow. "See ya tomorrow morning."

Evelyn nodded and headed back toward Andel's classroom, while Autumn ran after the guys. Andel had some explaining to do. If he thought she asked a lot of questions before, he was in for a shock. She thought of a question to go with each stride, all the way down the hallway.

"Why was Tate so blah towards me?" Evelyn said after she opened the door. "You frickin' made me look like every super-nerd's fantasy. All I was missing was the cape. He should have been flirting hard core."

"That is why we are here." One second Andel sat in a chair on the front row of the class, then their surroundings flickered to their apartment's living room. Andel landing on the floral, overstuffed couch looked like a bull sitting in a field of sunflowers.

"Hellooo, *poofin'* code word!"

"Sorry. It has been a while since I have had to work with another Cupid."

"Speaking of Cupid-things, when Jeremy and Autumn met, it felt like I swallowed a subwoofer. Is that normal? Did you feel or hear it?"

Evelyn stepped over to a decorative mirror in the entryway. Brown hair fell over her shoulders, and brown eyes surrounded by long, thick lashes peered behind her. She could see Andel in the reflection with a hand stroking the stubble along his chin.

Andel's assignment was to teach Evelyn the ways of the Cupids, but he wanted to avoid information overload. He'd fed her bits and pieces at each training session. At first, she appreciated the bite-sized portions. As time went on, though, she began asking more questions about getting her Cupid powers. Going with her gut instinct had to be a part of the process.

"It is good that you picked up on Jeremy and Autumn. I experienced a draw toward them, but they could be your first mark if you felt something."

"Something? Try a herd of somethings." Evelyn's arms flung wide open. "This whole thing is exhausting. I need chocolate."

"It is settled then. They will be your first *connection*."

"That's a new term for the handbook. Is there more to it, or are you being vague on purpose?"

Andel crossed one leg over the other, getting comfortable. "Evelyn, when will you ever just accept things and stop asking so many questions? Wait. Don't answer that. I know it will come in the form of another question. If you come over here and sit down, I'll try to explain."

Evelyn crossed the room and plopped into a blue reading chair across from Andel. The pillows were more firm than she anticipated. When she didn't sink into the seat, it reminded her of the clouds she rested on in the Heavens. She slipped off her black ankle boots and pulled her knees up to her chest, settling in for one of Andel's lectures.

"Lay it on me."

"When your arrow successfully pierces two hearts, the couple will connect. But you will also be linked to them. We are warriors, ready to assist love and fight for it. Over the years, our numbers have dwindled because so few humans are willing to fight for love. Your sacrifice made you special, Evelyn. Few would give up so much for another. A love that pure is what is required from Cupids to share it with mortals."

"So, you're saying I'm a love warrior linked to humans who couldn't care less."

"I was hoping to come across more eloquent."

"Your wordiness is lost on me. I'm a woman of action."

"I remember. You took a speeding streetcar to the face if I recall your actions correctly. You should know, all Cupids have been made by their actions."

"Really? So what did you do? You couldn't have been run over, they didn't have cars back then. Did they?"

"I died pulling my wife and kids out of our burning home."

"Oh." Evelyn slowly set her feet on the floor. "I'm sorry."

"It was a long time ago. My point is that we are all called to action, to fight. The most difficult part of our job is waiting.

Once we feel called to unite two lives, we have to be patient and make sure they are in perfect alignment. Once our arrow is shot, we must be willing to fight for their love. Sometimes that means fighting alongside them to keep that love alive."

"Why couldn't my Cupid have kept *me* alive? I wouldn't be annoying you, and Tate wouldn't be an emotional zombie."

Andel took a deep breath. Silence replaced the gravity in the room. It wasn't until Andel spoke that they were both anchored.

"Evelyn, you cannot hold on to the past, but you can fight for Tate's future. The two of you shared a true love, but it was young and new. Over time, our connections fuse together. If love matures and grows, the two hearts we bond become one. That bond strengthens our own power to connect others. The message the Elders gave us is about a warning about something beyond the Veil. Darkness is threatening to extinguishing immortality and our other abilities. It all has the Elders *quiver*ing in their boots."

The lame attempt to lighten the mood was lost on Evelyn as she focused on the task at hand. Maybe if she helped the Cupids out, they'd give her some extra time with Tate. "Then, I guess I'll have to get that arrow so we can make the offering."

"Yes, you will."

"One last thing, if I take the arrow from Tate will he be able to find true love again?" Evelyn had hoped their love would last a lifetime. Living for an eternity as a Cupid, she figured the closest she would ever get to love again would be when playing matchmaker.

"That's up to him."

Chapter Three

"How in all that is holy did I miss again?" Evelyn's cherrywood bow clattered against the pavement. A moment later, her empty leather quiver landed next to it.

Andel shrugged and opened his mouth to answer.

"Shut up. If you make a *hole* joke at my expense, I may just stick you in the eye with one of my arrows."

"You have no arrows left to shoot," Andel chanced, pushing Evelyn's buttons, as he took a step closer. Dry leaves crunched under his boots. The two had agreed on a late night training session in the shadows of Jackson Square.

"You're a giant, smug, smart…"

"Evelyn Bowden."

"If you want to make me flinch try *Evelyn Diana Bowden*." Evelyn's voice shrilled. Eerily, she sounded like her foster mother's would have if she'd left her dirty dishes on the counter. There wasn't much to miss from that part of her life. She'd left for college and never looked back.

Andel perked up at the sound of her middle name. "There is no excuse Evelyn *Diana*. Your namesake was that of a Greek goddess known for her ability to hunt. Now, climb into the tree to retrieve your arrows. I will wait." Andel knew something would eventually spark in her. Evelyn's inner desire to aim with precision and spirit would soon consume her.

"Yeah, right. If you plan on making me scale that tree, you better intend to be my next target."

Andel stood, more motionless than the oak behind him. The stance was a test of patience, but Evelyn couldn't figure out if it was for him or her. So, she picked up her bow and quiver, trudged to the tree, and began climbing.

In a matter of seconds, Evelyn had pulled five arrows out of the copper and gold foliage. Her powers were maturing, but she fought distraction. She could tell something was different the moment she woke up in the Heavens. She wasn't human anymore, but she wasn't immortal yet either.

"Do you think I'll be able to pull this off?"

"Hitting me with an arrow?" Andel stretched his arms out, making himself a larger mark. "No. Maybe if I placed a chocolate pie in the tree, you would have a chance." He stood at least eighty feet away.

She knew she could hit him, but she'd rather eat the pie. Being back on earth, everything tasted better, especially dessert. "What? You're an idiot. You don't think I'm really going to try and shoot you?"

"Why not? I am the one that is immortal."

Once, Andel explained to Evelyn she would become immortal after she pierced two hearts. But she wasn't sure she really believed him. Evelyn jammed the wooden practice arrows into her quiver one at a time. Gripping the last one in her hand, she shouldered the container.

"You are, aren't you…?" Evelyn stretched her arm out in front of her, with her bow parallel to Andel. A gust of humid air blew her hair behind her shoulders. Pulling the string, she increased the tension to ensure her arrow would travel the distance needed. She wasn't sure if she was crazy, but she released the silver-tipped weapon.

Faster than a kid swiping candy at a convenience store, Andel's hand whipped up in front of his chest. He'd snatched the arrow out of flight. The arc had been solid, and if he hadn't caught it the point of the arrowhead would have penetrated Andel's breastplate.

"Perfect." Andel's compliment surprised Evelyn, along with the fact that he'd just transcended two feet in front of her. He handed her the arrow.

Evelyn didn't ask why he chose such a rigid, archaic style of gear to train in. Maybe he was getting into warrior-Cupid-mode or he simply enjoyed wearing stiff leather gear.

"Perfect catch, you mean? You're really messed up. What would have happened if my arrow hit you?" Evelyn asked, She had a feeling the arrow would've bounced off his medieval breastplate.

She preferred a more breathable fabric and wore a green cotton tunic with leggings and boots. Leather seemed to be a prerequisite in every Cupid's wardrobe. Evelyn sported a wide leather belt that helped with her posture and accentuated her waist.

"A better question is, what were you feeling when you shot it?"

"Hmm... Let's see." Evelyn struck her best Andel-thinking pose. "Annoyed, frustrated, pissed, confused... Need I go on? What does it matter what I felt anyway?"

"What you feel will be struck into the heart of your target, Evelyn. Our arrows are not meant to kill, but death might be welcome to someone struck with maliciousness or agony."

"So if I actually hit a human with my arrow, he or she would be cranky for the rest of their life? That's brilliant. I feel sorry for the guy who chose me for this gig, I bet he's getting ripped a new one by the Elders right about now."

"I am sure he is not sorry for choosing you, Evelyn. You need to see the beauty and honor in what we do. I remember being in your position and how difficult it was to see past the grief."

"How long did it take you? I mean, how long was it before you struck a couple with true love?"

"I will admit, I was not expected to recover as quickly as you. But my love was more different, more developed than your love for Tate."

Evelyn began to shake her head in irritation. "Developed. *Developed?*"

"Please, let me explain." Andel took Evelyn by the hand. His arrow tattoo shimmered and sent a calming warmth through her. Emotional manipulation was a new ability for her to file away with all the others. "You and Tate were shot with a Cupid's arrow a few months before your untimely death. Your love for each other felt monumental because it was meant to be."

Evelyn knew Andel spoke the truth the same way she knew Tate was special when they met. She didn't feel the need to make sure he was a good kisser before committing to a second date. Tate made her feel beautiful inside and out. She had wanted to be consumed by that love for the rest of her life, and technically, she had.

"Go on," Evelyn encouraged Andel. She hoped something he said could take away the ache that throbbed in her chest.

"I fell in love with Theodora when I was sixteen. We courted for three years, and I served two of those years in the military. After receiving our parent's blessings, we were wed. The world was different. To feed our growing family, I reenlisted. Five years of marriage went by in a mixture of bliss and torment, but we fought for every joy. I lost my life after rescuing my two children and Theodora. The worst part is, as a result of the fire my sons lost a battle with a fever. Then, Theodora died less than a month after they died."

"I'm not sure what to say."

"You do not have to say anything. I did not tell you so you would feel sorry for me. I want you to understand it is possible to find it in you to fight for love again."

Evelyn wasn't as alone as she felt. Andel's resolve soothed her discomfort for now, but as soon as she faced Tate again the pain would return. Evelyn wondered if Andel was really past what happened in his life. She knew better than to rip that Band-Aid off.

"When I was with Jeremy and Autumn, I felt hope. Not even Tate could distract me from wanting the two of them together."

"That is good. Really good. Speaking of Tate, did you happen to notice anything different about his appearance?"

"No, well, nothing except for the not being attracted to a bombshell thing."

"That is what I thought." Andel began unbuckling one of his shoulder straps. "You must exercise patience. Piercing Jeremy and Autumn's hearts this early in their relationship could cause it to be based on a physical foundation." Andel's eyebrow quirked, trying to insinuate what he would not say out loud.

"What? Do you mean sex?"

Andel cringed and quickly started working at the buckle on his other shoulder. "It is one of the most common misunderstandings in today's culture. What you need to remember is that there are more factors that you must consider before you go off shooting your arrows at complete strangers."

Evelyn giggled more at Andel's awkwardness than the unintended pun. The conversation did remind her of one her father tried to have with her when she was twelve. That talk was instigated by a boy in her class who'd asked to meet her after school. Evelyn's dad explained that each kiss she gave away couldn't be replaced. Someday all her kisses would tell her love story. She was a sucker for a good love story, and her dad knew it.

"Ok, then. I'll wait. Maybe I can befriend Autumn and get some details to help Jeremy. You know, her dream date or something? The problem is we may not have enough time."

"Let me worry about time. And since there are more pressing matters, I suggest we focus on trying to get you close enough to Tate to remove his arrow."

Evelyn closed her eyes, imagining herself in Tate's arms. Would she have to get *that* close? No. She couldn't put herself through connecting with him, only to be forced to transcend back to the heavens. She had to focus on the task at hand. Opening her eyes, she met Andel's gaze. "I know what the mission is, but I was less than four feet away from him earlier today, and I didn't see any arrow. How close are we talking?"

"You know there can be nothing romantic." He looked down at the floor. "I did get a glimpse of the arrow as he stood near me. Tomorrow morning, you may try to sit next to him. I have a theory I am working on, but I do not want to get ahead of myself."

"What does the arrow look like? Is it like this one?" Evelyn held up one of her practice arrows.

"Every arrow meant for true love is made of pure gold."

"It won't have blood and guts on it, will it?"

"No, Evelyn." Andel's mouth turned down in disappointment. "We have been over this. It is a magical instrument used to affect its targets, not maim them."

"I hope it doesn't hurt Tate when I pull it out."

"I honestly do not know if it will. In all my years, I have only delivered true love, not taken it. Mortals have been known to break the bond themselves. It is painful in more than one way, but there is not one account I have heard when love was removed by a Cupid. Consider this, if his half of the arrow is removed, he could have a chance at love again. We will also be able to continue our work. You know you want to spend an eternity looking at this face."

"Did you just try to make a joke?" Evelyn got the feeling things were more serious than Andel let on. He rarely joked about anything.

"See if I ever try again." Andel pouted. "You should get some rest. Let's go."

Chapter Four

The scent of coffee beans and sugary pastries filled PJ's Cafe. Tate and Jeremy occupied a table in the back of the restaurant, both hunched over laptops. Evelyn took a deep breath, refusing to let memories of the place overtake her. She'd spent many late nights studying and early mornings caffeinating here. Most of them with Tate.

"Cordelia!" Jeremy noticed Evelyn first. Or, he noticed the glamour Andel had shrouded her in.

Evelyn had prepared to be called Cordelia, but she looked forward to being able to drop the alias after the mission. The last thing she needed to deal with was an identity crisis.

"Look who decided to show up." Tate glanced at his watch.

It was 9:02 am. She would have shown up earlier, but she'd had to convince Andel to let her go to the study session alone. He'd tried to persuade her to let him sit across the room and pose as an elderly man. She argued that the pressure would be too distracting. She had to try to get close enough to Tate to remove his arrow, and a chaperone wasn't necessary.

"Sorry, I couldn't decide what to wear." Evelyn cringed at her half-truth, because Andel chose to cloak her in a turtleneck. She wouldn't leave their apartment until he changed it to something more age appropriate. A compromise was made and she eventually left sporting a college T-shirt.

"Typical," Tate muttered at his computer screen. "I'd like to get started, Jer. Are you sure Autumn is coming?"

"Yeah, Man. Relax. We have the professor's aide here to help us. This is going to be awesome!" Jeremy focused on the windows facing the street as if to look for her.

"So other than Human Behavior, are you guys taking any other minimesters before Christmas?" Evelyn asked.

"I'm only planning on *taking* Autumn out."

"That was lamer than lame. You have reached a new level of pathetic," Tate scoffed. He pulled out a textbook and let it thud against the tabletop.

"The only thing lame around here is you. Autumn was texting me for an hour last night, and you're just jealous."

"Whatever."

Tate went back to tapping keys on his keyboard, and Evelyn sent a tight grin in Jeremy's direction. If she couldn't get Tate to open up, maybe she could work on earning Jeremy's trust.

Evelyn couldn't forget retrieving the arrow from Tate's heart was her number one priority. But, number two on the list was waiting for Jeremy and Autumn to find love. Evelyn figured it wouldn't hurt anything if she helped things along.

"So what did you two text about?" Evelyn was sure the two were attracted to each other. Leaving it all up to a text message typed with the wrong emoji could ruin Jeremy's chances with Autumn.

"Well, I checked to make sure she was coming, and then she replied 'I find your lack of faith disturbing.' The force totally brought us together."

"What? You lost me." Evelyn didn't think humans knew about Cupids.

"Jeremy called Autumn out on her geeky Darth Vader reference. They texted nerdy to each other for the rest of the night," Tate interjected. He didn't look up, missing the confused look on Evelyn's face. She hadn't gotten the Star Wars reference, and she hadn't pegged Autumn as a fangirl.

"She's brilliant," Jeremy said. He wore a toothy grin, not taking his eyes off the front door.

"I hope so, because we're going to need a miracle to pass this class. Have you read through the syllabus? We have to read through Chapter Two: The Multidimensional Framework for Assessing Social Functioning."

"How are you going to assess someone's social activity when you don't have any to speak of?"

"Hey. I'm here aren't I?" he shrugged.

"Ummm… I hate to break this cute banter up, but how about we get started?" Evelyn suggested. If she didn't steer the conversation into something more positive, Tate might decide the constant quips from Jeremy weren't worth sticking around. "If you play it right, you can help catch Autumn up during our first break."

Jeremy shoved his laptop over to make room for Evelyn. She pulled out a textbook with an identical cover to Tate's. The difference was where Andel had highlighted passages. He'd explained she would need to go over the notes with the group.

The idea of existing without the need for sleep appealed to Evelyn. Andel had used the ability to prep for Evelyn's meeting, but Evelyn thought she'd rather catch z's. Once she sealed pierced her first couple, she'd become immortal. Staying awake forever wasn't as cool as being able to transcend anywhere.

Evelyn flipped through to the second chapter. She asked, "You've each read Chapter One, right?"

"About that..." Jeremy began.

"I have, but lover-boy was texting instead of reading last night, remember?" Tate finished.

"I probably shouldn't tell you this, but Dr. Lambros will be quizzing over the first two chapters this afternoon."

"Why did I let you convince me to take this class, Tate? God, this is torture. We should be enjoying our Christmas break, not practicing social dysfunction."

"Give it a rest, Jeremy. There's no reason to hash this out in front of Cordelia. Or would you like me to explain why we're having to take this course in a minimester? Two weeks of cramming isn't worth adding an entire semester to the end of our program."

"Please." Jeremy folded his hands like he was praying. "I'll stop, just don't go into a monologue about life and death. Your droning on rivals Dr. Lambros."

"Nothing is as mind numbing as Andel's lecturing." Evelyn immediately caught her mistake. She didn't have to see Jeremy's raised eyebrows or Tate's pinched lips.

Autumn's perfect timing and wide smile signaled that she'd heard the slip up as well. "You two are on a first name basis, huh?"

"Ewww... He's old!" Jeremy went from stunned to grossed out in less than two seconds.

"He's hot. Like 007 hot," Autumn defended.

"Whoa." Evelyn pushed the thought of Andel's hotness away with two hands up in the air. "First, Dr. Lambros is my mentor. The first name basis has been earned with study and hard work. Second, he is handsome and older and so not my type."

"That was second, third, and fourth. I'd also like to add that only the first of those reasons was an adequate defense. I'm not convinced." Autumn pursed her lips at Evelyn.

"Now that we've wasted precious brain cells trying not to picture that, can we please get back to studying?" Tate glared up at them.

"Tate, did you just hear yourself? It sounds to me like you've arrived in Lameville." Jeremy laughed at his own joke, while Autumn grinned at Evelyn. Autumn's eyes shot over to Jeremy as she ran her finger over a silver bracelet wrapped around her wrist. It resembled bones. Evelyn thought she must have seen it wrong.

"I agree with Tate. Let's get this done. Some of us still have to read Chapter One," Evelyn defended, and rose an eyebrow at Jeremy.

It took Evelyn forty-five minutes to explain the terms and ideas that Andel noted in her textbook. None of the others stopped to ask questions. They scribbled notes down and highlighted sections in their own books. Evelyn hoped that if the study group went well, they'd want to meet up again. But if she could encourage Jeremy and Autumn to hang out outside of class, their friendship would grow into something more, faster.

"Thanks again for your help." Tate packed his things up and headed for the exit. Evelyn followed, leaving the other two in a fit of laughter.

"You're welcome." She stepped outside into the muggy air. "Wait up. Why are you off in such a hurry?"

As she caught up and matched his gait, Evelyn noticed the stubble along Tate's chin. His skin was pale and eyes sunken in. He didn't look like himself or the guy she knew and loved. He was more miserable looking than the low-hanging gray clouds.

"I don't want to be around when Jeremy gets his heart broken."

"What makes you think that'll happen? Maybe he and Autumn are meant for each other."

"Nah. I don't believe in happily ever afters."

"Really?"

"Really." Coming to a corner, a car zoomed by and Tate flinched. It was typical New Orleans traffic.

"Well, if you ever need to talk, I'm around." Evelyn extended a smile to Tate.

"Thanks, but I'm good." He started to turn away from her, but hesitated. "What makes you think I need to talk about anything anyway?"

Evelyn looked down at Tate's chest. Blue cotton stretched over his lean muscles, but there was no sign of an arrow. "I don't know…"

"You're right. You don't know." Tate stiffened and walked away from Evelyn across the street without another word.

She stopped herself from going after him. Hounding him wouldn't open him up. In fact, reaching out to him would lead to a worse reaction. So, Evelyn walked in the opposite direction to the apartment. She wasn't getting anywhere with Tate. Cold doubt crept through her jacket into her bones.

A chill shook her as light rain began to fall, brushing against her face. She stayed on the sidewalk, darting under balconies most of the way along Chartres Street. She traipsed past cafes, tourist traps, and voodoo shops. Something about the city had intrigued Evelyn from the first time she visited. That was back when she was a senior in high school. Everything back then had felt so alive.

Since coming back as a Cupid, she felt the intrigue in a new way. She recognized the life, but she also thought she perceived death. The darkness couldn't quite hold her, but cold loss brushed against her arms. As she passed the street to turn to her apartment's entrance, St. Louis Cathedral came into view. Its grandeur and timelessness pulled her closer. The cathedral pointed to something bigger than herself, and she approached the front doors. She had the feeling someone was watching her.

Stepping inside, Evelyn wasn't sure what to expect. The ceiling and its never-ending arches fascinated her. Wrapped her arms around herself, Evelyn felt death's pressing weight slip away. The church refused the darkness entrance. Any doubt she let bubble up on her walk slowly waned.

"Evelyn?" Andel's voice echoed in the chamber.

"Yeah, it's me," She assured. It was no surprised to see Andel in such a holy place, but she wasn't sure she belonged. Evelyn was full of fight lately, but somehow she knew love was at the root of her resistance. "I won't explode or anything in here, will I?"

"Of course not. What brought you to the cathedral?"

"I'm not sure. I'm not sure about a lot lately. I don't think I'm going to be able to retrieve the arrow. Tate won't even talk to me about your class, let alone open up about how he's feeling. He got all awkward and left when Autumn and Jeremy started flirting. Then when I tried to ask him about it, he might as well have built the Great Wall of China between us. Guys are ridiculous!" Her last word reverberated through the church and a robed man stopped pacing between pews, looking up at the two Cupids.

"I think you're missing something obvious. Remember, men are not complicated. Tate must have felt something if it compelled him to leave so hastily," Andel said. He placed a hand on Evelyn's shoulder. She shrugged at his weak attempt to console her. "Let's take a stroll back to the apartment. I think we have a few things to go over." Andel nudged Evelyn toward the exit.

"Please, not another lecture."

"No, a Cupid-lesson. I think it's your turn to learn something about human behavior."

With a sigh, they left the building. Outside, the ominous vibe she'd felt a few minutes ago was gone. The sun had appeared and so had more tourists. Jackson Square buzzed with people. Andel didn't waste his time with a cloak today, Evelyn would be hidden in plain sight.

As they walked, Andel tensed once, then twice. Evelyn wasn't sure what was going on with him until she was hit in the gut with nausea. Her stomach clenched, but she kept moving.

They were being attacked.

Andel's pace sped up, and Evelyn jogged to keep up with him. Her queasiness subsided, but Andel still had an arm bracing his stomach. He winced with each step. Evelyn figured the onslaught must be immortal. There was no way the divine chocolate cake from earlier could've turned out this evil.

"Come this way." Evelyn raced in front of Andel and pulled him under a balcony and into an art gallery. "What's wrong? Are you okay?" She didn't understand why he was still in pain. They slowed down, and Evelyn pretended to peruse the swirl of color on the wall.

"This is better, thank you." Andel leaned into Evelyn. His weight caused her knees to buckle. She knew they couldn't stay in the gallery without someone noticing there was something wrong with him.

"There has to be an exit in the back. Let's head that way. Then, you can poof us back to the apartment."

"I'll need a few minutes to muster up the strength." Andel limped, putting his weight on Evelyn with every other step. She gritted her teeth as they shuffled toward the exit sign that hung over a doorway in the back of the room.

"What's the matter? I mean I think I felt a fraction of what attacked us, but do you know what caused it?"

A metal bar secured the door along the back of the room, and red letters warned 'Emergency Exit Only.' If they pushed through it, someone could follow. Looking out a window to her right, Evelyn figured they could walk out into a typical New Orleans street. While filled with people and shops, she wasn't sure they'd blend in well enough. Andel needed to rest, and her best bet was to get him to their apartment or back to the church. Both were too far away.

Circling an exhibit of bronze sculptures, Evelyn noticed a few people staring at Andel. She was about to risk an escape through the alarmed back door when a large statue caught her eye. Another door, slightly ajar, hid behind a gleaming monstrosity. A plaque next to the statue read *Dragon*. The beast stood six feet tall with scales that reflected track lighting. Evelyn took a step closer and noticed an 'Employees Only' sign concealed behind the creature.

"You know, those are real." Andel tilted his head in the direction of the art piece as they studied it.

"What? You're delusional." Evelyn scanned the employee break room, and it appeared to be empty. "Sit here. You need to tell me how to make you better. Can I get you something?"

The break room was small. A thread barren couch lined one wall while a kithenette lned another. There weren't any windows, so they could hide out until Andel felt better. When a refrigerator hummed to life in the corner, it startled Evelyn.

"Come sit down. It will pass." Andel patted the brown cushion next to him.

"What's *it?*"

"A witch most likely doing a love spell in the square. They probably did not know to look for a Cupid this time of year."

"Why would a spell affect you this way?"

"Not just any spell. A love spell to activate a love potion. It's a quick fix for mortals, but it doesn't compare in power to love's arrow."

"But you're immortal."

"Think of it like a type of virus. Love can come in different strains, and Cupids only deal in the purest form of love. We thrive on true love when we are near it. When a different form of love is around, it can have different effects. Most strains don't harm us, but fake or false love weakens us. The witch doing that particular spell was strong."

Evelyn had a difficult time getting her mind around all she was hearing. After weeks of training, she'd thought she wouldn't need Andel much longer. His current condition made her realize how unprepared she was. Sitting down on the overstuffed couch, she couldn't put much distance between them because of Andel's size. Her head fell back on a beige pillow.

"Why would a witch be doing a love spell in the middle of a bunch of tourists? In the middle of the day?"

"It could have been a performance, but my best guess is that it was personal. The Oak Moon can give more power to witches when they are near oak trees. The square has some of the oldest oaks in the city."

"Okay. Oak Moon. Check."

"Evelyn, the Oak Moon is significant in many ways for the witches…and for us."

"Why's that?"

"Our mission." Andel hunched over, placing his elbows on his knees. "There is a deadline."

"Big shocker. Do I also have to remove Tate's arrow blindfolded?"

"No, Evelyn. Be serious for one moment." Andel let out a long breath. He'd been debating whether it would be a good idea to tell Evelyn the truth.

"How long do I have?"

"*We* have until the Full Oak Moon." He leaned back into the couch and nudged Evelyn with his arm. "*We* can do this."

Evelyn let her head fall over onto Andel's shoulder. She would need his help to accomplish this feat. Her heart hadn't been in the mission so far. It was crazy to think that Andel's existence hinged on her success. He'd been trying to protect her, but was that helping her?

"A witch *could* have been doing a spell, but could it also be that I'm an epic failure? Our offering is still stuck in Tate's heart!"

"We will retrieve it, Evelyn." Andel reached for her hand. She didn't have time to flinch, and she didn't want to pull away. She watched as their fingers interlocked.

Andel lifted her chin with his other hand and made eye contact. Her skin was as warm and comforting as her brown eyes. Someday, he would tell Evelyn all he saw in her. She was different.

Andel decided not to hold back any more, at least when it came to the truth. Evelyn was perceptive and intuitive, and she could handle it. Finally grasping the gravity of their situation, she would fight for their kind. Evelyn exuded the same fierceness of the oldest and strongest Cupids.

"We have two weeks."

"Are you freaking kid…"

Poof.

Chapter Five

Appearing in their apartment, Andel and Evelyn softly landed on the couch. Andel knew he ticked Evelyn off once again. He'd transcended without the courtesy code word. The stabbing pain in his gut had subsided. He had been able to build up the energy to *poof* them out of the art gallery's employee lounge. Pillows hugged the two Cupids making it difficult for Evelyn to push herself out of the fluff.

"Adieu. Sayonara. Arrivederci. So long." Determined, Evelyn struggled to unravel her fingers out of Andel's. His hand impulsively gripped tighter. With a thud, his arm fell to his side in the space she'd been sitting.

"I apologize." Andel planned to stay calm and brace himself for Evelyn's outburst.

"Your apology is *not* accepted! I can't believe you, poofing us to the apartment when I should be trying to get the arrow from Tate and acting like two weeks isn't a big deal!"

"You can do this, Evelyn. I did not want to tell you about the Oak Moon and its phases because you tend to digress whenever I go over anything new." Evelyn's mouth fell open at Andel's accusation.

Andel and the other Cupids looked like angels when Evelyn first woke up in the Heavens. She'd fallen into a catatonic state when she found out they were Cupids. But who wouldn't be stunned at the idea of Cupids being real? He explained she would become one of them, an immortal being, and that's when she'd really lost her grasp on reality. She had lost everything when she died. And, to top that they wanted her to spend an eternity giving away something that was ripped from her. Evelyn sobbed for what felt like days.

"I guess I should be thanking you for keeping me in the dark?" Evelyn asked darkly.

"That's not what…"

"You know what? Thank you. Thank you for teaching me archery and poofing me back to New Orleans and making me confront my ex-boyfriend, who I haven't even grieved for yet. Thank you for evading the truth of the full moon *dead*line and keeping me somewhat in the loop when the balance of good and evil is being threatened. It's no biggie if I fail and we all have to face Hell on Earth. I'm sure it'll work itself out." Evelyn folded her arms across her chest and rolled her eyes.

"Are you finished?"

"Let me think…" She paused, then scratched her head and rolled her eyes. The silence crawled over Andel and made him twitch. "How about we make a deal? You quit with the protective dishonesty, and I'll work on the task at hand and save the world."

"Deal," Andel agreed. "Class will begin soon, and I propose you make an effort to schedule another study session."

"I don't think that's the way to Tate's heart. Tonight, after you assign a special project, I'll ask him, Jeremy, and Autumn if they want to study after class."

"Special project?"

"Yep, we are going to need an excuse to go down to the Quarter and study *Human Behavior*." Evelyn quirked her fingers in an air quote, and grinned.

Chapter Six

Tate walked next to Evelyn. She posed as Cordelia Hunt again, and didn't know it was her under the glamour Andel implemented. Jeremy and Autumn had coerced Tate to join them in the French Quarter. He didn't put up too much of a fight because *Professor* Lambros' latest assignment. They were required to observe people and their actions in a public place. When Jeremy invited Evelyn, she knew it was to keep Tate from feeling like a third wheel.

"Does this place ever shut down?" Tate looked out over the crowd. His jeans appeared baggier than normal. The wrinkles in his shirt rivaled the lines that strained across his forehead.

They'd met up in front of Hotel Monteleone, and Evelyn longed to reach over and hold his hand. She shouldn't and couldn't. Tate had shoved his hands in his pockets and avoided eye contact.

Crowds formed in front of bars and voodoo shops and didn't thin out much between. Instead of fighting the throng of bodies, Evelyn was able to twist and weave her way down the block. She didn't miss how Tate bounced and knocked into people with his head down. Her heart clenched at the notion of Tate beating himself up over losing his true love.

"Tourist trap." Autumn looked over her shoulder at Tate and glanced at Evelyn with a raised brow. During the walk, the new couple, Jeremy and Autumn, had drawn closer together like magnets. Evelyn, a.k.a. Cordelia, and Tate had been pulled further apart.

"How long have you lived here, Autumn?" Evelyn asked. Autumn had to be a native to New Orleans. Her bohemian-broom skirt swished over the street and her layered bracelets clinked against each other. Autumn fell in accord with the city and towed the others like luggage.

"All my life. Not always in the Quarter, but my family owns a shop down here."

"One of the voodoo shops?" Jeremy asked with a grin. "I knew you cast a love spell on me."

The pick-up line brought a smile to Autumn's face. "Actually, we own a cafe over near Jackson Square. We make the best étouffée in Louisiana." Autumn straightened her shoulders with pride. Her family's Cajun restaurant was easier to fess up to than her family ties to magic.

"That's brilliant!" Jeremy reached out and took Autumn's hand in his.

The gesture caused Autumn's smile to widened.

Evelyn felt like butterflies swarmed inside her chest. Tate winced. Then a pack of loud 20-somethings barged between their party. The group ripped Autumn and Jeremy apart, but Tate instinctively pulled Evelyn to him. The rowdy bunch would have trampled Evelyn if he hadn't swept her to the side. Delight filled Evelyn, but regret immediately took its place.

"Excuse you!" Tate hollered over his shoulder at the passing mob.

"It's okay. Really." Evelyn tried to console Tate, but he continued walking. The only thing that compelled Evelyn to follow him was the hint of jitters in her core. It wasn't because Tate saved her from being trampled. Autumn had reached back over, taking Jeremy's hand in hers.

The foursome planned to walk along Bourbon Street and then choose a bar or club based on which one was the busiest. They agreed to take mental notes and share them after an hour or two of observing.

The universities in town were on Christmas break. In any other city, cold weather might keep students at home and the tourists in their hotel rooms. Not in New Orleans.

The streets smelled musky, but not as pungent as in the hot summer months. Each building had its own life, distressed and colorful. The tourists could be spotted a mile away—guys wearing too much cologne and girls not wearing too much of anything. Evelyn was thankful for her jeans, boots, and leather jacket. It wasn't cold but cool enough that the humidity felt like a wintery-wet blanket.

Autumn paused in front of a set of ornately carved wooden doors. "How about this one? It won't be overrun, but there will be plenty of people to watch."

The place felt powerful, supernatural. Not gut wrenching, but haunted. It made Evelyn's skin crawl. She thought she saw another layer of glamour, or maybe magic, lying in wait underneath the nightclub. As the giant doors opened, cathedral like windows were revealed. Evelyn could see strings of lights dangling over the dance floor. Colored lights swirled from a stage and the club bounced, filled with bodies and bass.

"You know, this is my third year at school in NOLA and I've never noticed this place." Jeremy gawked over his shoulder at the slew of people in line.

"I might know a guy." Autumn winked at Jeremy and strutted up to one of the bouncers. He looked over her shoulder at her three new friends. Jeremy and Tate exchanged glances, and Tate shrugged.

Autumn turned and waved them in, while the Andel-sized security detail stepped aside. They hadn't been carded, which was almost disappointing to Evelyn. Andel had used some of his Cupid-mojo to create Cordelia Hunt an I.D.

The sound of electronic music pulsed through Evelyn as she stepped inside. Her nerves felt exposed and sensitive to the buzzing interaction. The heightened emotions weren't normal, but they weren't bad. She followed Autumn through a level of high-top tables and a haze of smoke. They stepped down a short staircase onto a second level with the stage and dance floor. Bodies moved to the music throughout the room. Autumn grabbed Evelyn's hand before a couple could separate them. A whisper of power stretched itself from Autumn around Evelyn's arm. Sucking in a sharp breath, Evelyn froze in surprise.

"What was that?" Evelyn yanked her hand back and bumped into Jeremy who had been walking behind her. Autumn didn't bother answering. She probably hadn't heard the question or felt the jolt. Autumn just nodded to the other side of the room and kept moving. They climbed a set of stairs and Autumn pushed a red velvet curtain aside, wrapping it behind a hook. She revealed small room overlooking the club with black leather couches.

"Guys, please make yourself comfortable. Cordelia and I will be right back." Autumn didn't wait for a reply or take a drink order. She hooked her arm around Evelyn's and pulled her toward the bar. They passed a mass of people ordering drinks and flirting. Arriving at a door labeled *Ladies Room*, Autumn pushed her way inside.

"Who are you?" Evelyn didn't stop to check for inhabitants.

"Who am *I*? Who are *you*?" Autumn bent down to look under the four stall doors. "I know you're not quite human, so just 'fess up. Are you a shifter? I know you're not a witch, or I'd have recognized you even with that glamour."

Evelyn stood stunned with her back against the wall. She expected Autumn to explain that she was the owner's niece or something. Obviously, Autumn knew supernatural creatures existed, but how had she known Evelyn was using a glamour? "A shifter? Like a werewolf?"

"Yeah, well, I mean a shifter can change into any number of animals. Wolves do tend to be more prominent around these parts, but you'd know that if you were one."

"Autumn, I'm not sure…"

"I'm a witch," she blurted. "Not a normal one or a powerful one, not really even practicing. But with a family like mine, there are expectations."

Evelyn allowed an awkward pause to linger. She tried to calculate what she could reveal to Autumn without sending Andel into an outrage. Giving up the truth about her inclination toward Autumn and Jeremy was a bad idea. Evelyn wasn't fully a Cupid yet, but she knew it would be easier to stick close to the truth. The word *hypocrite* flashed across her mind as she thought back on how mad she'd gotten at Andel this afternoon. He'd been trying to protect her the same way she wanted to protect Autumn.

"I'm a Cupid-in-training."

"A Cupid? Really? You guys are so rare! My grandmother mentioned meeting a Cupid when she was young, but that was like a hundred years ago."

"Technically, I'm not a Cupid yet. I'm here on a mission to earn my proverbial wings."

"Wow. Is there anything I can do to help? I mean, I'm sure you don't need help, but if you need anything, just let me know."

"Thanks. I'll keep that in mind."

Autumn's enthusiasm and her connection to witches could prove helpful. So, Evelyn decided to enlist Autumn. If witches could impact Cupids the way Andel had been attacked that afternoon, it would be important to have one on their side.

Evelyn sighed and leaned closer to Autumn. "I'm here to help Tate."

"Jeremy gave me a little backstory about him losing his girlfriend last year. No wonder he's such a prickly thing."

"Do you think you can keep Jeremy occupied, so I can get to the root of what's really wrong with Tate?"

Autumn placed her hands on her hips and took in Evelyn from head to toe. "Sure, but I don't think your glamour is Tate's type."

"I'm not trying to be his *type*. I'm trying to help him get past his dead girlfriend. In a platonic-stop-being-depressed way."

"Sorry. I guess I was thinking of a succubus."

"Succubus. For real?"

"Yep, and they are crawling all over this town. It's the perfect feeding ground."

"Please, don't feel like you have to explain. I'm on information overload." Evelyn raised a hand and measured the amount she'd learned that day to be about two inches above her head. "How about we get back to the guys?"

"Sounds like a plan."

Walking back to the swanky VIP room, Evelyn noticed the crowd continued to grow. The buzzing power in the room also grew. Watching a blonde sit next to a single guy at the bar, she wondered if either of them were supernatural. Evelyn hoped becoming a Cupid included some sort of paranormal radar in addition to becoming immortal.

Jeremy and Tate sat down on separate couches. They sprawled themselves out, sitting like they were watching Monday Night Football. Not witnessing paranormal creatures let loose in a dark nightclub.

"Hey!" Autumn bounced up to Jeremy. "Come with me." Her smile was all he had eyes for, and when he took Autumn's hand Evelyn felt their affection for each other. It was different than the feeling that tingled over her skin when they first walked in. That was on the surface, and this feeling filled her heart.

Evelyn plopped down beside Tate, hoping he wouldn't clam up or leave. "So… Human Behavior. What do you think you'll focus your assignment on?"

"Since we're surrounded by a bunch of people trying their hardest to make a good first impression, I'll probably center the paper around that."

"Good idea. Are you good at reading people? I mean, are first impressions important to you?"

"They're important, but they aren't everything." Tate looked over the crowd. "Take that guy over there in the purple dress shirt. He's trying way too hard. Since I sat down, he's hit up three tables of girls here for Bachelorette parties."

"I totally agree, but maybe he's lonely. At some point a person gets so lonely they become desperate." Evelyn turned to face Tate, but he continued to avoid eye contact, his arms crossed over his chest.

"I guess."

Evelyn tensed, knowing she must have said something that hit too close to home. Tate was beginning to shut her out. From experience, she knew he didn't dance, nor did he hang out at clubs. He was also guarded, even more so than she remembered. She needed to keep things light.

"Want to try an exercise?" One of Tate's eyebrows quirked at Evelyn's question. "A Human Behavior exercise that focuses on nonverbal cues."

"Sure. Why not?" Tate relaxed and waited for further instruction.

Evelyn took in the people meandering around the tables closest to them. She spotted a guy with bleach-bond hair and a leather jacket making his way to a young brunette in a tight blue dress. "Those two." She pointed.

"What about them?"

"You get to make up the dialogue for the girl, and I'll create the male's side of the conversation. But you have to use a girly voice."

"Okay…" He straightened to get a better view.

"Ahem." Evelyn cleared her voice and started talking an octave lower as the man began to talk to the woman. "You look cold. Want to use me as your blanket?"

The woman eyed the man up and down, and as her lips began to move, Tate jumped in. "If I wanted some guy to use a lame pick up line on me, I would have stood over there." Tate's dialogue fit perfectly as the woman pointed to the bar.

"Right, but I didn't want to waste my lameness on any of those girls." Evelyn snickered and waited to see what the guy would do next. "How about we start over? I'm not sure why you're standing here all alone, but I'd like to keep you company."

The woman shook her head and turned away from the guy. Tate's voice disrupted Evelyn's concentration. "Nah, I'm good. Better off alone." The man shuffled away with his head hanging. The rejection was heart wrenching to watch.

"Is that how you feel Tate?" Evelyn scooted a few inches closer to Tate on the couch. "It's not true. You deserve to be happy."

Tate leaned over and came eye to eye with Evelyn. He searched her face as she sat frozen, worried he could see through her glamour. The notion that he knew who she really was scared her more than elated her. If he knew she still existed he'd never let her go.

His face darkened as he clenched his jaw. "I *was* happy." Tate stood up and walked away.

It was true. They'd both been happy. She knew how heartbreak left her wallowing in loneliness. Now, as a Cupid she had purpose, and the grief had distracted her.

Before Evelyn could pull herself together to go after him, he was on the opposite side of the dance floor. In the corner of her eye, she noticed Autumn wrapped in Jeremy's arms. An overwhelming urge to pierce them with one of her arrows took over. Standing, Evelyn lost sight of everything and everyone in the room. Her bow and quiver materialized at her side and she began to mentally prepare for the shot. Picking up the arrows, they looked a different from the ones she had practiced with. If they'd been conjured by her developing powers, she assumed it had to be the right time to shoot.

As Evelyn pulled her bow up parallel to her posture, a strong, heavy hand gripped her shoulder. She hadn't had a chance to see how the arrow in her hand transformed from silver to blazing red. She'd been distracted by Andel.

He'd wrapped one of his arms around his stomach in pain.

"Adieu."

Chapter Seven

"Did you really think they were ready?" Andel's question didn't surprise her. He'd want her to have a spreadsheet and diagram to prove they were ready. Instead, she'd reacted to the urges that invaded her senses at the club.

"Why wouldn't they be? Are you okay?" Evelyn's bow and arrow were no longer in her grip, but her arm was still extended as if she were aiming. Andel's hand moved across her arm, and the weight guided it to her side. He was no longer in agony.

"I'm fine. And you better know why they are not ready unless you miss my lectures and need a refresher."

"Just gouge my ear with one of your arrows now." Her heart still raced with the adrenaline of aiming her arrow, but the electricity that had buzzed over her skin had begun to fade.

"They will be ready soon, but you must be patient."

"Waiting is not a strength of mine. I guess I thought if I couldn't get the arrow from Tate I could at least do something right and pierce Aut-emy."

Andel's face scrunched up in confusion. "Aut-emy?"

"It's their couple name." She avoided having to explain by walking to the living room and splaying herself over the couch. "Never mind. I'm too tired."

Andel followed then reached down and lifted Evelyn's ankles. He sat with her feet laying over his legs. "Soon, you will not miss sleep."

"I hope it's because I'm immortal and not because I've screwed everything up and ended up in Hell."

"Evelyn, it does not work that way. I know you want to sleep, but how about some archery practice? I think it will make you feel better."

"I don't know." Evelyn wanted to escape, and sleep seemed like the best option.

"Did you notice how your bow and arrows appeared when you mentally summoned them? I think you need to start training with Cupid arrows. The oak ones are usually for practice, and you will find shooting with a golden arrow is *different*."

"Okay, but when I'm ready to come back, we *poof* back. No nagging or extra shots."

"Agreed."

In an instant, Andel had transcended them to a forest with a canopy of green foliage. Evelyn inhaled salty air. No gulf, ocean, or sea was in sight, but as she took in her surroundings she noticed targets mounted to tree trunks as far as she could see. They were different sizes of red rings, hung at various heights.

"Where are we?" Evelyn adjusted her leather belt. Andel had changed their clothes into a more traditional Cupid fashion.

"My homeland, Greece."

Evelyn's mouth gaped open. She'd never traveled out of the country. Never having gone further than two states away. "You *poofed* us to Greece?"

"I like to come back here to train. Welcome to Maratha." Andel pointed toward the grove of trees before them. "Try summoning your bow and quiver, but think of arrows made of love."

"Huh?"

"I know it sounds cheesy. Just try."

Evelyn's forehead wrinkled in concentration. She envisioned her long, sleek bow made of oak and it materialized at the foot of a tree a few feet away. The quiver was harder to picture. She closed her eyes and made sure to imagine several silver arrows filling the quiver.

Before she opened her eyes, she crossed two fingers for luck. She wasn't sure anything had happened, but resting next to the bow was a quiver full of metallic arrows. They shimmered with power.

"Nice job." Andel already gripped his bow with his gloved hand, and his quiver was strapped across his broad back. "At the end of the course, you will find the cliffs. Follow me."

Andel set off. He darted from one tree to the next doing a summersault. He'd picked an arrow from his quiver while in motion and crouched down. Quicker than Evelyn could clearly see, he had aimed and shot his weapon. A thud sounded from forty feet away, and she could see a glint of silver between two branches. An impossible shot for a human to make.

Evelyn strapped on her quiver and picked up her bow. This live-action training exercise was going to be epic. Adrenaline coursed through her body as she sprinted under a low-hanging branch and pulled her bow up. Reaching for an arrow, she then swiftly pointed it and released. Her arrow gleamed in the light that broke through the leaves above. It struck its target an inch shy of a bull's-eye. Bewildered at her ability to see so clearly, she rushed to cover behind another tree. Halfway to her destination she pulled a second arrow and shot at a target equally as impossible as the one Andel had just hit. Flying between two limbs and past a mark that would have been much easier to hit, the arrow took an outrageous left. Its head drove into the center red circle.

The perfect shot, impeccable eyesight, and healthy competition propelled Evelyn through the forest. She hit every bull's-eye she shot at. Striking each mark hit a sweet spot in her subconscious, and she didn't want the feeling to end. A clearing opened ahead, and Andel stood under the last target. Beyond him a cliff opened up to crashing waves.

Evelyn's momentum powered her into the clearing. She spotted Andel's arrow at the center of the target and yearned to better him. Reaching for the nock of her last arrow, Evelyn drew and anchored it. Her heart skipped a beat when Andel shifted in her peripheral vision. The arrow in her hand flashed red, and she was flooded with passion.

"Whoa! Andel, what's happening?" Evelyn screamed when the transformed arrow pulled her at her core toward Andel. Her desire to hit the target was overpowered by a need to shoot him. The feeling wasn't malicious, but warm and inviting.

"I am not sure." He shuffled to the right, testing if Evelyn would also change direction. The arrow didn't relent but steered her. "Drop it!"

"I'm not sure I can." The red arrow pulsed brighter the closer she got to the hulking Cupid.

"You can. You have to focus on something other than the warmth."

"Warmth? Do you mean the desire I have to pierce your heart with love?"

"Yes!" Panic hitched Andel's voice an octave higher. "Think about rodeo clowns or unicorns or something!"

"Rodeo clowns?"

"Evelyn, focus! Make sure you picture whatever it is clearly."

Her pace slowed as she imagined a bull bucking at Andel while he wore a painted smile and red nose. The arrow faded from red to its silvery hue. Evelyn came to a stop a few feet away from Andel, and he seized the arrow from her bow. His chest rose and fell, heaving in relief. The adrenaline that had previously pumped through Evelyn wore off. Her shoulders slumped and tears welled up in her eyes.

"I was going to hurt you, wasn't I?" Her bow clattered on the ground. "There is something seriously wrong with me."

"No. You are special, Evelyn." Andel walked to the cliff's edge. "I have heard stories of a Cupid that lived thousands of years ago. A Cupid who fought for the love of the immortals."

"Is that a thing?"

"It is rare for immortals to find love and practically impossible for them to have their love protected by another immortal. There is too much jealousy, rivalry, and hostility."

"But how do you know my arrows are meant for immortal love? What if I had shot you and it turned you into a zombie or something?"

Andel chuckled at the idea. He had lived for a couple hundred years, and even the necromancers he'd met knew better than to summon the dead after a certain amount of time had passed. "The Cupid who lived long ago had a *fiery* touch. Seeing your arrows turn red, I can only guess they were referring to red arrows." He shrugged his shoulders.

"Why?" Evelyn stepped up next to Andel, watching the crystal blue water crash into the rocks at the base of the cliff. "Why me? What's different about me?"

"Where would you like me to start?" In a flash, the back of Evelyn's hand smacked Andel's arm. He hadn't stopped her. He couldn't. She was growing more Cupid-like, more immortal, with every training exercise.

While she transformed into an indestructible Cupid, she still had concerns. She swallowed her worry, but one tear escaped, leaving a wet trail down her cheek. She wished she could be as unbreakable on the inside as she felt physically. "What if I'd hurt you? Or, let's say for kicks that it was an arrow for immortal love. Who would you have fallen in love with?"

"Remember, I am immortal. A luminescent red arrow would have the same effect, I think, but I could catch it before it pierced me. If I was unaware of the shot, a silver arrow might break the skin and leave me feeling flirtatious for a few hours. Nothing to worry about." He thought, *at least for now.*

"I like how you avoided answering my questions about it turning red and who you'd fall in love with."

"I did not avoid it. I was merely trying to think up a good way to tell you that I could have fallen in love with you. There is no way for me to truly know."

"Pfft! With me?" Evelyn took an awkward step away from Andel. "But wouldn't it have had to pierce both our hearts? We don't even like each other all the time. I mean you're not that bad looking or anything, but you kinda talk a lot, and you're bossy. Plus, you *poof* me to random places, are super-serious all the time, and never use contractions."

Andel's eyebrow rose into his hairline, and his lips twisted in thought. "You are partially correct. We have discussed how a Cupid's arrow must puncture two human hearts for the pair to be joined in love. The tales told about immortals are more vague. It has been thousands of years since an account has been given. The stories have most certainly altered over time."

"Get to the point, already."

"The rumor is that long ago, when an immortal was struck by a fiery arrow, they were granted eternal love. It only makes sense for the one struck to fall in love. I do not see how an arrow could be strong enough to pierce two immortals. It would seem that all the Cupid-cartoons your culture enjoys are more relevant to what occurs when one of us is struck. It could be dangerous if the feelings are not reciprocated."

"If I'd shot you, you could have fallen in love with me. But I wouldn't have fallen for you?" Evelyn crossed her arms over her chest. "It would have gotten awk-o-taco really fast, but why would it be dangerous?"

"Think about shooting a vampire and filling them with passion, then said vampire lays eyes on a werewolf. It would lead to war, and every immortal race would be forced to pick sides."

Andel's example forced Evelyn to consider what would happen if her new friends were pierced. The two seemed like average college students.

"What if I had to shoot a mortal, and hmmm… a witch?" Evelyn bit her bottom lip trying to keep herself from expounding.

"Are you referring to Jeremy and Autumn?"

Evelyn gasped. "How did you…?"

"I noticed your arrow's color at the club. I brought you here to make sure my assumptions were correct."

"The arrow changed at the club?"

"Yes."

"Ugh." Evelyn kicked the dirt.

"What?" Andel couldn't stand any straighter or be any prouder that he was right.

"Are you ever wrong?" Evelyn's arms swung up, and she waved him off. "Wait. Don't answer that. Let me guess. You think I was called to shoot Jeremy and Autumn because of my unique situation?"

"Technically, Autumn is not immortal. As a witch, there are other issues that would keep one of our normal arrows from having the desired effect. But, yes, your special abilities will allow immortals the same love we are able to give humans. You will have to be very disciplined, Evelyn."

"Blah, blah, blah. With great power comes great responsibility." Evelyn pointed a finger at Andel as if she could teach him a lesson.

"Yes. That is a poignant realization for you to make."

"Just call me Spiderman."

Andel's face cringed in what could only be terror. "Why would you want to be called Spider-anything?"

"Do I detect a phobia?"

"I might have a healthy fear of the spawn of Satan, but I think it is time that you faced your fear."

"Sounds like fun." Evelyn deadpanned and started back the way they had come. She searched the trees for arrows. They had all vanished.

"It is a perk." Andel nudged Evelyn with his elbow, falling in step beside her. His touch sparked a warmth that hugged her heart, a feeling she missed so much that it throbbed.

Ignoring the discomfort, Evelyn nudged Andel back. "So have you ever cliff dived?"

"Yes, but you are not ready for that." He ignored the same pinch of unease and smirked at her. "But you might be ready for a race," he goaded.

"Go!" Evelyn yelled over her shoulder at him as she trudged into the forest.

Chapter Eight

The next few days went by in a blur. Evelyn played the part of Cordelia Hunt perfectly—helpful, intelligent, funny, and platonic. She spent every morning studying with Tate, Jeremy, and Autumn. Every afternoon, they sat in class listening to Professor Lambros drone on. In each lecture he dropped hints about how an individual's past could determine their present behavior. Evelyn figured he was doing his own part subliminally.

With the end of the Human Behavior minimester on the horizon, their final loomed over them like a dark cloud. Evelyn, glamoured as Cordelia, and waited for Tate at their coffee shop of choice. They'd always been in a group setting, but today she knew she needed to make an attempt to retrieve his arrow.

"Thanks for calling, Autumn." Evelyn was sitting at a table for four, talking on her cell. Tate approached with a wave. "Yeah, I'll see you later."

"What's up?" Tate asked as he pulled out his computer.

"Autumn just called to let me know that she and Jeremy are going to be late."

"How late?"

Evelyn had actually asked Autumn to distract Jeremy for a few hours so she could make her move. "Like, meet-for-lunch-late?"

"Ugh." Tate started to push the screen of his laptop back down. "I was hoping to get a little feedback from them."

"I'm sure you'll have time to run things by them before class, but maybe I can help quiz you this morning."

Tate paused and glanced at the steaming coffee in front of Evelyn. "Are you sure?"

"Of course. If there's anyone who can help you impress Professor Lambros, it's me." Her cheeks warmed when she heard herself. "That came out wrong. Just get out your notecards."

"How did you know I have notecards?"

Evelyn knew how Tate studied. He had used notecards while they were dating. "Doesn't every college student use notecards?"

"I guess."

"I was going to suggest that we make some if you didn't have any." Evelyn tried to recover. She pulled out her copy of the textbook and opened it in front of her. Then she dug around in her messenger bag for a stack of blank notecards and a pen. "If you miss any, there will be consequences."

Tate smiled, accepted the challenge, and handed his deck over. "I'll get you a refill of coffee for every five I miss."

"Deal!" Evelyn's love for the rich, black java had confounded Andel more than her addiction to sweets.

The first round was the easiest. Evelyn read the definition on the card, and Tate had to remember the word it matched. Tate sucked at tests and had missed seven out of thirty when they took their first break. Evelyn needed another cup of joe, and it gave Tate the opportunity to look over his notes before round two.

The cafe was getting busier, and Evelyn meandered around a few groups before sitting back down. Tate was engrossed in his work, unaware of the chatter echoing around them.

"So, Tate, what do you want to do with your life?"

He looked up, blinking twice before answering. "Um. I'm not sure."

"Why take Lambros' class if you might not even need it?"

"Long story." Tate shuffled his papers into a neat stack. Evelyn took a sip of her hot coffee and waited. And waited.

"Fine. I wanted to work in social services, but I'm not sure about it anymore."

"Why?"

Evelyn met silence. Tate didn't understand why he felt compelled to share, so he fought the inclination.

"Sorry. I didn't mean to pry," Evelyn apologized.

"No. I'm just not good with people lately."

"Okay…" Evelyn hoped the discomfort of silence would elicit more sharing.

"The Human Behavior class is a last ditch effort. My girlfriend died last year. We were doing this together, but I don't know what I want to do anymore."

His admission crashed over her like a wave reaching the shore. Before he could pull away Evelyn had to try and reach him. She understood how lost he felt because she had felt the same way before she found a purpose. Tate needed to be reminded of what started him on this path. "Did you want to get into social work before you knew her?" She knew the answer, but he had forgotten it.

"Yeah. I was adopted when I was a toddler. My adoptive parents are amazing. But, the transition into their family may not have been possible if it weren't for my social worker. I've always wanted to be able to help other kids like me. So did Evelyn."

Laughter bubbled over from the next table. Evelyn didn't want to hear any more. She didn't need to be reminded of the system she was bounced around in as a child. And, unlike Tate, she didn't have wonderful adoptive parents to reflect on. Her goal was to find kids that got lost in the system and find them a home.

"You know, I think you could ace this final if you try."

"Oh, really? I know I can." Tate leaned forward and snatched the notecards out from in front of Evelyn. She was flustered, but searched his chest. Nothing. It was all green T-shirt and 'Tulane' stretched over muscled pecs. As he settled back into his seat, he caught her staring.

Instead of blushing, Evelyn challenged him. "You should put your money where your mouth is. If you fail, you know you have to take this class again. That is, unless you quit the program, but you don't seem to be a quitter to me."

"Go on."

"If you ace the final, I'll put a good word in for you with Andel."

"So you're back to a first name basis?" Tate raised his eyebrows.

"Ugh, I'm so glad I didn't say that in front of…"

"Me?" Autumn piped up. She'd been standing behind Evelyn for a few seconds. "What do I get from *Andel* if I ace the final?"

"*Ahem,*" Jeremy interrupted.

"Don't worry, honey, I'll work you into the deal too." Autumn patted Jeremy on the butt as he walk around the table. "Please, tell me y'all are ready to ninja-kick this test in the teeth."

The squad breezed through a round of flashcards. Then Evelyn had each of them expound on phases of behavior because she knew they would be included in an essay question on the test. Getting through the material was difficult since all Evelyn could think about was how she would fail the Cupids. She couldn't see the arrow, and without it, they would all be doomed. While Tate and Evelyn packed up, Jeremy and Autumn rushed out of the coffee shop.

"Hey, thanks for the pep talk earlier." Tate shoved his laptop in its padded sleeve.

"Pep talk?"

"You know, reminding me of why I'm doing all this."

"You're welcome."

"See you in class." Tate threw his bag's strap over his shoulder and left without another word.

Evelyn followed him onto the street, but turned the opposite direction. Her steps were sluggish. When she got to the apartment she would have to tell Andel. Passing the entrance to the Pontalba Building, she was drawn in the direction of the cathedral again.

As Evelyn turned into Jackson Square, Andel appeared *poof-*style inside the rod iron fence. "Are you avoiding me or the task at hand?"

"Only you." Evelyn walked to a nearby oak. Andel followed, but didn't interrogate her. "I didn't see it. I'm not a Cupid and maybe I'm not fit to be one."

"Slow down." The two were concealed by a low-hanging branch. Andel scanned the area for anyone that might overhear them. "What happened?"

"Nothing. And nothing is going to happen. I couldn't see it. I'm not a Cupid, or I'm just not meant to be one. Don't you think if I were, I'd be able to see that stupid arrow in Tate's heart?" Her jaw clenched and hot tears leaked out of the corners of her eyes.

Andel peered out across the square, leading Evelyn to believe he dejected her. "I have an idea."

"What? Are you going to offer me up as a replacement?"

"No. Do not be ridiculous." Andel faced Evelyn, and his stony brow softened. "Oh, Evelyn, I am sorry, but there is no time for you to be…"

"I know, I know, we have a week at best."

"No, I mean you need to summon your gear." Andel looked over his shoulder at the crowd swarming around the fountain at the center of the square. "Now."

Evelyn closed her eyes and pictured her bow and quiver. The quiver appeared strapped to her back, and her bow materialized in her left hand. Andel was impressed by her determination and hoped his idea would work. He had spotted Jeremy and Autumn sitting on a bench in the middle of a pack of tourists.

"You are going to pierce your first hearts."

"Are you kidding me? What if they're not ready? What if I'm not ready?"

"The fact that you were concerned for them before yourself is all I need to hear to know you are ready. Nock your arrow and let it speak to you. Let Jeremy's and Autumn's hearts sing to you."

"Why now?" Evelyn pulled an arrow from her quiver.

"Maybe we have been at this backwards all along. If you are a Cupid, you will be able to see Tate's heart and the arrow buried inside."

"How do you know? Can you see his arrow?"

"No. I can see the other half, the arrowhead that was once attached to it, in your heart."

Chapter Nine

"An arrowhead. In *my* heart?" Evelyn began in a low voice. "I'm dead, Andel. I'm training to be a Cupid, an immortal being. How can an arrowhead be stuck in my heart?"

"It is not impossible."

"No sherbet, Sherlock!" Evelyn raised her hand to her lips. "What the f-fritter?" She wasn't sure where between her brain and mouth her explicit words were transforming into sweet treats, but the result was baffling.

Andel chuckled, unable to keep his lips in their unbending line. He knew he was right to have Evelyn shoot Jeremy and Autumn now, but he would have to wait to explain. They didn't have time. Jeremy got up from the bench and was reaching for Autumn's hand.

"You have got to take the shot." Andel pointed to the couple.

"But I'm blurting…"

"Take. The. Shot."

Evelyn smacked her lips as she raised the arrow up to her bow. It began to change from silver to red before her eyes. Jeremy had taken Autumn in his arms. The love he embraced her with and the heart she entrusted to him filled the square with music. Evelyn felt their growing love in her own heart and knew it was the perfect moment to join them to each other.

Pulling the nock of her arrow back into the bow's string, she kept her arms level and released. "Oh, God," Evelyn whispered, hoping and praying her arrow would hit its target. It darted through the air, glinting in the sunlight. When it collided with Jeremy's back Evelyn expected him to shudder in pain, but the shaft dissolved. Evelyn thought she noticed the two pull together closer as the arrow struck them.

It had struck them both. Then everything flashed stark white. It was whiter than white, and Evelyn felt weightless and warm for a moment.

"Whoa!" Evelyn blinked away some spots and turned to Andel. She pulled another arrow out of her quiver with Cupid-speed. "That felt unbelievable, but don't think you're off the hook. What the h-honey is going on! Why can't I fudging cuss?"

"Welcome to the club." Andel smirked. "How about you not point that at me considering what happened last time?"

"Fine."

"As a Cupid, you will enjoy the perks of transcending and many other powers. You will also be held to a higher standard."

As Evelyn brought the bow and arrow to her side, she noticed a shimmer along her forearm. An arrow tattoo had revealed itself. The arrowhead had a shaft stretching a few inches, and a singular line made up the fletching. It looked like Andel's, but hers was more delicate. The thin, fine lines looked more like jewelry.

"A tattoo? This I'm good with. Am I really going to be able to be a Cupid with an arrow encased in my heart? Why didn't you tell me about it earlier?"

"I knew you were ready for your first shot when you started shouting desserts at me. Some of your Cupid powers started to show themselves, like agility and speed, but the sweet-speak convinced me you were ready for the transfiguration."

"And blurting brownies is an immortal superpower?"

"Not quite. Because each of us began as a human being, we each have a few vices. As a reminder that we are not perfect nor all-powerful, our cries of anger recall our greatest weakness."

"Good grief, I've turned into a sweet-toothed-Tourette-syndrome Cupid."

"You also have the ability to transcend anywhere on the earth, glamour yourself to look like anyone or thing, and you can heal. That is all in addition to speed, agility, strength, perfect aim, and those immortal arrows you shoot."

"Yeah. Did you notice the arrow pierced both Jeremy and Autumn?"

"Yes. I wasn't sure if it would affect both of them, since Autumn is a witch." Andel ran his hand along his chin.

"I wonder what would happen with two immortals."

"We will have to worry about that later."

"Okay. Hey, do you ever exclaim desserts?"

"No. My vice is not the same as yours, but I have one. Just like I once carried an arrowhead in my heart. Eventually, you will have to remove it."

Evelyn didn't like the idea of the arrow being removed from her heart. She had felt stuck since her first day in the Heavens, and now she knew why. It started out as a comfort. Then, it began to bind her to the way things used to be.

"I'll worry about that after I've offered Tate's arrow and saved our supernatural race. How do you suppose we can make that happen?"

"How tired are you?"

Evelyn wasn't tired at all. In fact, she'd never felt better. Andel thought it a good idea to get the arrow tonight if it was possible. The pain that had occasionally incapacitated him was attacking him more often. It meant that they needed to make their sacrifice sooner than later. Andel had come up with a plan, and Evelyn perfected it since she was able to *poof* without Andel at her side.

They waited until late evening. The first quarter Oak Moon shone over the quad in front of Tate's dorm. Evelyn hadn't ever been inside, so trying to transcend into his room would be too risky. She and Andel *poofed* under a tree standing just outside an area they thought to be Tate's room. A quick call to Autumn confirmed the room number and assured them that Jeremy wouldn't be back any time soon. She also arranged for Tate to leave their door unlocked for Jeremy. It was tougher to correlate the room number with the right window on the third floor.

Before opening the front door, she glamoured herself invisible. Evelyn looked over her shoulder at Andel. He was the only one who could see her. He nodded, signaling that Tate's light had gone out, and she used her Cupid speed and agility to enter the building without being detected. As Evelyn climbed the stairs, she went over the plan in her head.

She couldn't simply take the arrow from Tate's heart in his sleep. That was too easy. He had to relinquish it. Evelyn would glamour herself in grayscale, like an Instagram filter, and wake Tate. She would pretend to be a ghost and try to convince him to move on. Once she had the arrow, Andel and Evelyn could make the offering. The only problem was Evelyn didn't know what would happen afterwards.

Slipping into Tate and Jeremy's room, Evelyn was able to make out Tate's bed immediately. She tiptoed across the room and added some iridescence to her glamour. The closer she got, the less convinced she was that this would work. Her disguise gave off enough light for Evelyn to distinguish a fletching. The end of the arrow usually depicted as feathers, was in plain sight. It appeared magically against Tate's bare, lean chest.

"Ta-ate," she sang. "Ta-ate."

He began to turn over, and Evelyn instinctively touched his shoulder.

"Tate, please wake up."

"Evelyn?" Tate blinked away the sleep and sat up, scrambling away from her into the headboard.

Evelyn stepped away from the bed to give Tate some space. "It's me."

"Is this a dream?" Tate rubbed his eyes and scanned the room searching for the smoke and mirrors that tricked his eyes.

"Something like that." Evelyn glided a half-step closer to the bed, but Tate flinched. "I've come to make sure you're okay, Tate. I know it has been difficult, but you have so much to look forward to in life."

"I'm starting to see that again, but I miss you." Tate let himself lean forward to get a better look at her. "Is it really you?"

"Yes. I miss you too, but you need to let me go."

"Why am I dreaming about you if I need to let you go?" Tate relaxed a little and shifted to the side of the bed. "I'm so lonely without you."

"But you don't have to be. I came to say goodbye, Tate."

He stood at her words, blocking her way to the door. "Please, don't leave. Not yet." He begged, but she wouldn't need the door to transcend. Tate didn't have to worry because she wasn't planning to leave without retrieving the arrow.

"Do you realize that I have to move on, too?"

"I never thought about it." Tate took a step toward Evelyn. "So I have to let you go so you can move on?"

Evelyn nodded her head, not willing to outright lie to him. She didn't know what it would take for her to get over him. With another step closer, she felt the warmth of his body. The hair on her arms stood up, and her senses were heightened. She heard his racing heartbeat and tasted the mint mingled with his breath.

"Can I touch you?" he breathed, reaching a hand out.

"I don't think that's a good idea." Evelyn inched back.

"Please."

Tate had never forced anything on Evelyn, and she yearned to hold him. Having him in her arms would only make it harder to let him go. He froze. Chin quivering, he shoved his hands into the pockets of his plaid pajama pants. Evelyn couldn't hold back. It would be the last time they laid eyes on each other.

"Okay."

Tate wrapped his arms around her waist before she could change her mind and pulled her close. His chest heaved with a sob. Evelyn felt her own eyes begin to tear up as she returned the hug. Her hands glided up his back, and an object materialized inside her palm. She encased the end of his arrow in her fingers and hid it from mortal sight with glamour.

Distracted by the appearance of the arrow, Evelyn was surprised to feel Tate's kisses along her hairline. Her relief and elation at finally having the offering encouraged her to kiss him back. One small peck on the cheek. When her lips met Tate's stubble, desire stirred inside her. She lingered a moment too long, and Tate moved a hand up to her neck. He pressed his lips to hers. The passion that consumed Evelyn took over. It wasn't anything she'd ever felt before. It wasn't human.

Evelyn couldn't get enough of Tate. Between kisses she ran her hands over his warm skin. Tempted, she wanted to let go of the arrow for a moment, so she could hold Tate closer. One hand roamed over his chest, down to the drawstring of his pants. He groaned with pleasure, and his fingers found their way to the skin under the hem of her top.

"You feel so real."

She could drop the arrow and be with Tate. If she did, the arrow and the Cupids would be lost. She had no clue where that would leave her or Tate.

"We can't do this." She stepped back putting space and clarity between them.

"If this is a dream, we can," Tate said with heavy eyelids.

Evelyn smirked. "You need to go back to sleep."

"But…" Tate reached for her.

"You were the love of my life, and that life is over."

"A part of me died when you did." A tear slid down his cheek.

"You will always be with me, Tate, but it's time to say goodbye. I'll move on if you will."

Tate nodded. "I will."

"Goodbye, Tate." Evelyn had held the tears back as long as she could.

"Goodbye."

Poof.

Chapter Ten

Andel straightened under the tree at Evelyn's arrival. His hand pressed against his stomach.

He wore a gray T-shirt and dark jeans, and almost looked like he belonged on the school grounds. His too-perfect complexion, statuesque build, and striking bone structure gave him away. The breeze caught his curls, but his hair wasn't nearly as disheveled as Evelyn's when she appeared. He would have asked about her tear-streaked face if it weren't for the arrow in her hand, and the wrenching pain in his gut. They needed to act soon.

"I need a chocolate chip cannoli."

"Did you just cuss?"

"Pfft… No. My mouth will only get sweet with you if I'm really mad."

"You should turn your glamour off." Andel winced as he crossed his arms over his chest. "Some college kid will see you, and rumors will spread about the campus being haunted."

"In this town, that wouldn't be such a bad thing. Are you okay?" Evelyn let go of the mirage, and her puffy lips went from gray to pink. Her tattoo glinted, and her mortal good looks surged into a legendary beauty.

"I'll meet you at the apartment," Andel's voice wavered before he vanished.

Evelyn, left alone in the cold brisk lawn, took the opportunity to straighten her shirt and run her fingers through her hair. She looked up at Tate's window. The lights were still turned off. He would wake up in the morning and believe it was all a dream.

Poof.

"Get your gear, Evelyn," Andel's voice echoed from his room. He sounded like he was back to full strength. "We have a cemetery to get to."

"You looked like you were holding yourself together back there. Are you sure you can do this tonight?"

"You will be the one doing the work. If we do not go, it will only get worse."

"Got it. So the Veil is in a place where people are buried? I guess that makes sense."

"I am not sure where the Veil is, but we will make the offering in a crypt at the St. Louis Cemetery. Who knows what we will come across, so we need to be armed."

"*What* we'll come across?"

"Vampires cannot enter hallowed ground, but as you know, in New Orleans, bodies are not buried in a typical fashion. We could encounter a wolf pack, skinwalker, or a dragon."

The crazy would never end. Evelyn had no idea how one of her arrows would fend off a dragon, but Andel hadn't led her astray yet. The two changed into Cupid armor, and Evelyn placed the end of Tate's arrow in her belt. They met back in the living room, and Evelyn wondered if she appeared as intimidating as Andel. She figured she came across more like his sidekick than a superhero.

"Do you want me to meet you there?" Evelyn knew the cemetery they were headed. There were a million places to *poof* within its perimeter.

"We will go together." Andel held out his hand.

Evelyn took it. No code words or qualms, she accepted the mission no matter the outcome. In a blink, she stood outside in the cold winter night. Vaults, white like ice, frozen in time, surrounded them. Andel took his time, approaching each doorway to read the family names. Evelyn expected to shiver while she waited, but Cupids didn't get cold.

"It is not this row. When I came to scout the other night, the crypts started to all look the same." Andel reached for Evelyn's hand again.

Evelyn closed her eyes, but instead of *poofing*, Andel pulled her between two burial chambers. "Where are we going?"

"I know it is close. We must find the correct door, enter the main chamber, and then, you will make the offering."

"Enter a chamber? These things are full of bodies." Evelyn patted a stone wall they passed.

"Okay. What's the name you're looking for? Maybe I can help."

"We are looking for a symbol."

The two Cupids were lights in the dark, two towers of strength. Andel stood with confidence, even in his tortured state. Hope surrounded him. Evelyn fought with her armor. She prayed it was the only thing she'd have to fight. Both of their weapons glinted in the moonlight.

The creepy-factor increased as they perused the older tombs. Each was surrounded by wrought iron and overgrown with vines. Evelyn wanted to find the crypt they searched for, but she wasn't going to risk getting lost. So she kept Andel in her line of sight.

"I found it," Andel called into the night.

Evelyn was two mausoleums away from him and jogged to meet him at the doorway. A set of iridescent wings glittered where a nameplate should be. An ominous feeling weighed on them both as they opened the door. It didn't creak. Bats didn't fly out. It was eerily quiet. The whole situation felt like they were in a horror movie. And, the new girl always got picked off first. If she succeeded, Evelyn would have to assist humans and supernatural creatures with their love lives for an eternity.

As they stepped inside the dank room, candles caught flame and lit a staircase. Cobwebs stretched along the ceiling. Evelyn gasped when a shadow disappeared into a crevasse in the corner. She swallowed a mouthful of thick, muggy air. The stone steps led down, but they couldn't see how far they went.

"I'll go first." Evelyn laid a hand on her hip where the arrow was tucked into her belt and proceeded to take the first few steps.

"Be careful," Andel offered, taking each step after her. "I am here if you need me."

Climbing down, the air became damp and cold. Evelyn reached the last step and suddenly stopped. Andel crashed into the back of her, forcing her into a foreboding chamber. Torches lit around the room one at a time. It was round and the perimeter was made up of stones covered in moss. At the center of the room, an ornate column stretched from floor to ceiling.

The column had an engraving, but it was incomplete. An ornate table covered with candles, dried herbs, and a large bowl stood between the Cupids and the fractured symbol on the pillar. Andel stepped around Evelyn and moved closer to the altar.

"I think you should put it in here." He pointed to the basin.

She wriggled Tate's half-arrow out into the open and set it inside. "I hope I don't have to sacrifice blood or anything with it."

"It only mentioned the arrow in the letter."

They watched the bowl for a few seconds. Evelyn was sure some magical swirling or churning would envelop the offering. She was ready to bolt for the doorway if it did. If someone else—a supernatural someone—appeared, she could shoot an arrow faster than a cowboy could pull his pistol.

But nothing happened.

"Did I do something wrong?" Evelyn was ready to take the blame.

"No." Andel paced for a minute. He settled in front of the symbol and studied it. He recognized an 'S' shape and a line crossing it diagonally. The bottom of the line looked normal, but the top was missing, along with a center piece. "Evelyn, if the altar does not accept the offering, it means we have the wrong piece of the arrow in the bowl."

"What are you suggesting?

"There is not much to consider. If Tate's half of the arrow does not work, then…"

"It's my half they want."

"Yes."

"What if I'm not ready to give it up?" Evelyn wanted to hit something.

"I think you are."

"My love for Tate is why I'm here! Wouldn't the powers that be want me to keep it?" she asked the dark ceiling of the chamber.

Andel stepped close to Evelyn and placed his hands on her shoulders. "Releasing the arrow will not remove your love. You will always have a place for Tate in your heart. The arrowhead inside you is only a symbol of that love. When you think about it, the message we received makes perfect sense now. *Bring the arrow which pierced two hearts, yet only remains in one.* The one that remains is yours to offer."

"But how?" Tears brimmed out of Evelyn's eyes, and she held her hands to her chest as if she could protect her heart that way. The arrow within throbbed, making it impossible to ignore.

"Simply let go. Concentrate on loving Tate so much that you want his happiness above your own." Andel wrapped Evelyn in his arms and let her cry into his leather armor.

As she imagined Tate fulfilled and thriving, the beating in her chest began to feel more like a stab. It hurt. The pain was so intense that she screamed. The echo of her wail bounced off the wall and sounded like a hundred screams. Her hands, still guarding her heart, were filled, and a sharp point pricked one of her fingers.

"Evelyn, I am so sorry," Andel soothed her. She had the arrow, but she let Andel's strong arms bring her comfort. In the silence, she felt thankful for this unlikely friend. She still had so much to learn, and she had hoped he would be the one to teach her.

"Thank you, Andel." Evelyn used one hand to wipe the streaks of tears from her face. She looked up and noticed Andel had let a tear escape. Of course, Evelyn knew he must have gone through the same thing. She'd hoped he had someone to help him the same way he held her together in this moment.

"Are you ready?"

Evelyn walked over to the basin and set her arrow inside. A metallic liquid slowly filled the bowl until it covered the arrow. The column behind the altar quaked, and pieces of gravel came loose from the ceiling. One of the stone symbol's missing pieces appeared in a glittery haze. It was an arrowhead.

"Do you think that's it?"

"Yes. You did well."

"*We* sure did!" Evelyn held out her fist. "Let's bump this out."

Andel's head tilted to the side. "What ever happened to high fives?"

"Never mind. Let's just get out of this creepy crypt."

"*Adieu.*" Andel grabbed hold of Evelyn's arm and they landed in the heavens.

"I wasn't expecting to poof here. No more New Orleans?"

"That is up to you. Where would you like to go?"

"I want to figure out why I'm different. Why my arrows can affect immortals and why I happened to become a Cupid when the Veil was threatened." Evelyn's determination would take her all over the world. She had an eternity to find the truth, but she'd need some guidance. "Andel, will you go with me?"

He smiled, ready to fight for love alongside Evelyn. "*Adieu.*"

Acknowledgements

Evelyn started out as a fun writing adventure with my Dynamis girls. Their constant creative encouragement and great advice had me writing this novella, as well as a follow-up novel. A special thank you to my cover/graphic designer, Drew Rodgers, and my editor, Maria Pease.

Finally, I want to thank the readers. Love is the real inspiration for this new series. I adore a good book, I obsess over characters who steal my heart and I cherish turning the page into a riveting world. Thank you for taking the time to read Evelyn. I hope you've fallen in love with Evelyn and Andel, and you can check out more in Unbreakable: The Cupid Chronicles (Book 1).

About the Author

Writing unique adventures with heart.

Kallie Ross has a passion for writing that has become an adventure in itself. She desires to create unique young adult fiction that incorporates legend, conjecture, fantasy, and conviction.

In addition to loving her life as a writer, Kallie adores being a wife, mother, friend, and teacher. She began her creative journey with books, a blog, podcast, and lots of caffeine. Ross never imagined her own adventure would be filled with so many wonderful people or words!

Read and learn more at KallieRoss.com.

Also by Kallie Ross

Unbreakable: The Cupid Chronicles (Book 1)

Dying for the love of your life...

Evelyn Bowden thought her story was over. Little did she realize, it had just begun.

The heavens made her a Cupid– a supernatural with the rarest ability. One that allows her to pierce both mortals and immortals with arrows possessing everlasting love. But Evelyn soon discovers Cupids fight a battle in a long fought war.

A duty to protect the purest form of love...

As Evelyn embarks on her first mission, helping a Gargoyle find his true love, she is exposed to the blurred battle lines between light and darkness. While an unknown threat proves it's willing to do anything to get their hands on Evelyn and her arrows, the heavens send Andel Lambros to help protect her. She finds herself at risk of being distracted by her former mentor, Andel, a stunning Cupid with dimples hard to ignore.

Missing her mark could lead to a supernatural war...

Having no idea how powerful she is, Evelyn is forced to put everything on the line as she balances the fate of the world on the tip of her arrow. But will love conquer all as once she hits her mark, or will all be lost in the end?

Descent: A Lost Tribe (Book 1)

Ollie Miller's summer has been socially miserable, but she's ready to leave all of the hurt feelings behind and move on with her life. When curious earthquakes begin to shake and rip open the foundation of her small town the ground becomes as unsteady as her feelings for her best friend, Mateo.

When they fall, they fall hard...

They descend into a cavernous wonderland that is both mysterious and breathtaking. Ollie, Mateo, Jesse, and Alexis just want to find a way back home, but instead they find Gabriel. He is a stranger to them, but he is no stranger to the labyrinth of caves underground. Together they begin a treacherous journey filled with ancient secrets, unexpected truths, and uncharted feelings.

Defend: A Lost Tribe (Book 2)

After emerging from her Descent into an uncharted underground world, Ollie Miller is sure of three things. First, her feelings for her best friend, Mateo, are far from platonic. She can't even look at Mateo without blushing at the memory of his lips on hers. Second, an evil man named Zadok is plotting to destroy the civilization above the surface. Third, there is no way to save the earth without returning underground. At least this time, she will have her mother along with Mateo and her friends to help guide her.

On their journey, noor, a mystical blessing guides them, but only if they're willing to follow. Ollie's determined to save the tribe from their evil leader, even if it means facing off with her long-lost grandfather. As Zadok comes face to face with his runaway daughter and his granddaughter, his plan starts to unravel, but is it too late to stop the destruction that he put into motion? Can the tribe survive and the surface be saved? Will Ollie learn to trust her own heart before it is too late?

Defend is the conclusion to Ollie's discovery of a lost tribe in Descent. Don't miss this adventure, brimming with ancient secrets and a thrilling underworld.